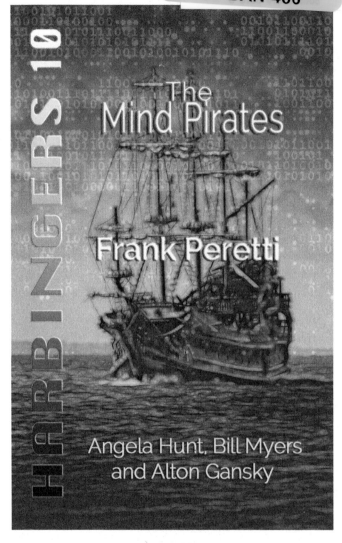

The Mind Pirates

Frank Peretti

Angela Hunt, Bill Myers and Alton Gansky

HARBINGERS 10

FRANK PERETTI

Published by Amaris Media International.
Copyright © 2015 Frank Peretti
Cover Design: Angela Hunt
Photos ©Ray8 and ©Priang, *fotolia.com*.

ISBN-13: 978-0692611807
ISBN-10: 0692611800

For more information, visit us on Facebook:
https://www.facebook.com/pages/Harbingers/705107309586877

or *www.harbingersseries.com*.

HARBINGERS

A novella series by
Bill Myers, Frank Peretti, Angela Hunt, and Alton
Gansky

In this fast-paced world with all its demands, the four of us wanted to try something new. Instead of the longer novel format, we wanted to write something equally as engaging but that could be read in one or two sittings—on the plane, waiting to pick up the kids from soccer, or as an evening's read.

We also wanted to play. As friends and seasoned novelists, we thought it would be fun to create a game we could participate in together. The rules were simple:

Rule #1

Each of us would write as if we were one of the characters in the series:

Bill Myers would write as Brenda, the street-hustling tattoo artist who sees images of the future.

Frank Peretti would write as the professor, the atheist ex-priest ruled by logic.

Angela Hunt would write as Andi, the professor's brilliant-but-geeky assistant who sees inexplicable patterns.

Alton Gansky would write as Tank, the naïve, big-hearted jock with a surprising connection to a healing power.

Rule #2

Instead of the four of us writing one novella together (we're friends but not crazy), we would write it like a TV series. There would be an overarching story line into which we'd plug our individual novellas, with each story written from our character's point of view.

If you're keeping track, this is the order:

Harbingers #1—*The Call*—Bill Myers
Harbingers #2—*The Haunted*—Frank Peretti
Harbingers #3—*The Sentinels*—Angela Hunt
Harbingers #4—*The Girl*—Alton Gansky

Volumes #1-4 omnibus: *Cycle One: Invitation*

Harbingers #5—*The Revealing*—Bill Myers
Harbingers #6—*Infestation*—Frank Peretti
Harbingers #7—*Infiltration*—Angela Hunt
Harbingers #8—*The Fog*—Alton Gansky

Volumes #5-8 omnibus: *Cycle Two: Mosaic*

Harbingers #9—*Leviathan*—Bill Myers
Harbingers #10—*The Mind Pirates*—Frank Peretti

There you have it—at least for now. We hope you'll find these as entertaining in the reading as we are in the writing.

Bill, Frank, Angie, and Al

Chapter 1

A BROKE BROKER

Adrian Pugh, Wall Street broker, offshore investor, and one-time multi-millionaire, paced nervously around his huge office, muttering, shaking his head in horror and disbelief. He turned and looked once again at the computer screen on his desk. The columns of figures and the totals at the bottom were still there. His first appointment was in ten minutes, and he would be eye to eye with one of the names on that computer screen.

After that, he'd be eye to eye with an arresting officer.

Outside the wall-sized windows, the skyscrapers of New York stood waist-deep in smog. The street was twenty stories below.

Twenty stories. More than enough.

Chapter 2

ANDI THE PIRATE

Adrian Pugh's intent was to end his life, but an awning broke his fall. Still alive, he would have to explain how millions of dollars suddenly vanished, not only from his own portfolio but from the portfolios of his clients. When he could not explain, the task of finding that explanation trickled down via the usual mysterious channels to myself and my teammates. The fact that we basically liked but could not stand each other had no bearing on the assignment we were given: to retrace Adrian Pugh's sailing vacation in the Caribbean on a 40 foot sloop.

McKinney here. James. 60, PhD, professor of philosophy and comparative religions, published, and so on and so forth, and no, do not be envious. Our sojourn on the crystal waters, verdant islands, and sugar-white beaches was strictly business, all eyes and ears to find a connection, if any, between Pugh's enchanting vacation and his precipitous loss. And let me add: A sailboat heeling in the wind with swanlike grace may appear romantic, but I assure you, the *Barbee Jay* was not roomy, especially with five aboard — especially *we* five.

Especially with Andi the Pirate at the helm, living in a world all her own.

"A stealin' scoundrel, a rogue I be,
from the Barbary Coast to the Caribbee,
to take in m'hand any gold I see,
with a hey, hi diddle and away!"

My red-haired, youthful assistant, you'll recall. I believe she composed the ditty herself. It went with the outfit: full, white blouse, thick leather belt and toy cutlass, baggy, striped culottes, a red scarf on her head, and a huge gold earring she'd bought on the island of St. Clemens.

"Ahoy there, matey! So you be sprung from the brig at long last!"

I'd just returned to the cockpit from a nap in the aft state room, not much different from sleeping in a drawer. "I was reviewing Pugh's itinerary. And sleeping."

"And now you'll be wanting a hand at the helm, I'll lay to that."

"No, go ahead. You're having so much fun — and what in the world are you singing about?"

She shrugged. "It's pirate talk."

Indeed. Adrian Pugh and family had taken in a raucous and touristy pirate show on St. Clemens, and so, keeping with our assignment, we took it in as well, and now . . . I could only snort with disgust. "Pirates! What sense does it make glamorizing criminals and reprobates?"

Andi looked up at the mainsail, curved and winging, and smiled as if seeing a vision. "Aye, but there lies the beauty of it. Stow away the rules and the makin' of sense and sail free!"

"Oh will you spare me!"

"What?"

"Armed thugs committing robbery on the high seas. Don't you see anything wrong with that?"

She wagged her head and rolled her eyes — as Andi, not Long John Silver, would do. "Ah, come on, it's the romance of it! Haven't you ever read Treasure Island? Or what about Peter Pan and Captain Hook? What about Pirates of Penzance?"

"What about 'stowing away the rules'? We're talking lawlessness here, aren't we?"

Oh dear. She gave me her studied look, a forewarning of debate. "Are you suggesting a transcendent morality?"

"You know I'm not."

"'Don't I see anything wrong?' That is what you asked me."

"The limitations of language, I assure you. There is no transcendent law because that would presuppose a transcendent Lawgiver, and of course *that*, my young lady, is the stuff of folklore and mythology."

"So how can the pirates be criminals and reprobates if there is no overarching scheme of right and wrong?"

Enough of this. I checked the compass as if she hadn't. "I believe our heading should be 070. Andi?"

7

She didn't answer. The big sloop began to turn toward the wind.

"Hey, careful. The sails are luffing."

The boat kept turning lazily into the wind as the sails went limp, flapping like laundry on a line.

"Andi, you're —"

She was leaning on the wheel, her eyes blank and her head quivering. "Aardvark . . . " she said.

"What?"

"Aardvark Basil Crustacean . . . "

I jumped up and took hold of her before she fell, easing her down to the pilot's bench. "Andi? Come on now, come back to earth."

Brenda Barnick's voice came from the bow, "What's going on back there?" With the foresail majestically to one side, she'd been able to lounge on the foredeck in straw hat, shorts, and halter, reading a book and looking like a travel poster. Now, fighting off the rude slaps of the foresail, she was groping her way back. Irritation gave way to concern at the sight of Andi slumped on the bench.

"Aardvark Basil Crustacean," Andi muttered, her eyes still blank and glassy. "Aardvark Basil Crustacean, 233 997 417709."

Andi was given to numbers, patterns, formulae. "Andi?" I said, "What are you giving me, a phone number?"

"233 997 417709."

"Anybody writing this down?" Brenda asked as she stepped into the cockpit.

"Execute, execute," Andi said in a monotone.

"Tank!" I hollered. "Bring a pencil and paper!"

"Aardvark." Andi's eyes began to roam. "Basil. Crustacean." She drew a breath, propped herself up.

"233 . . . 997 . . . 4177 . . . " Her eyes widened, she seemed to wake from a dream. "Zero Nine!"

She lunged for the stern rail and threw up over the side.

Tank came up the companionway to see the rest of us leaning over the railing. "Sick *again?*"

"Just Andi," I answered.

Ten year old Daniel was immediately behind Tank, all eyes as usual. Upon apprising the situation he backed down the steps into the galley, apparently to fetch something.

Brenda was still holding Andi, steadying her as she gripped the railing, gagging, coughing, gasping for breath. "Looks like a flashback."

"My fear exactly!" Her mind, so brilliant, so quick, had been sorely traumatized in our "fungus" adventure, deluded by the "emotional generator" we encountered in LA, hypnotized by a charlatan in Florida. After all that, I assumed we were witnessing a persisting damage.

"I'm--I'm OK," Andi said between coughs, spits, and swallows. She started to wipe her mouth on her puffy sleeve.

"No, baby, use this." With a praising smile, Brenda took a moist wash cloth from Daniel's hand and gave it to Andi.

"Was it a flashback?" Tank asked. I noticed he had brought a pen and scratch pad.

"I wasn't having a flashback." Andi turned from the stern rail and rested on the bench, wiping her face and drawing in deep breaths of ocean air.

"I'm afraid you were babbling nonsense," I told her.

"I know what I was saying!" she protested, and

wiggled her finger at Tank's scratch pad. He copied as she repeated quite lucidly, "Aardvark Basil Crustacean —"

"How do you spell crustacean?" he asked.

"Later. Fake it. Then there were numbers: 233 997 417709. That's A, B, C, and then some numbers, the same every time, even the spaces in between."

"But you were blanked out, as if having a seizure," I tried to counter.

She finished, "And then I said the word Execute. And then I said it again."

Now we all stared at her, waiting for the explanation. She only stared back.

"So what does it mean?" I asked.

"I haven't the slightest idea."

"How are you feeling now?" Brenda asked.

"Like I just puked. Where are we?"

"The Caribbean," I told her. "We left St. Clemens two hours ago. We were heading for St. Jacob. You were piloting the boat."

At that moment, Daniel squeezed around us and took the wheel, swinging the boat back on course. The sails filled, the boat gently heeled, and we started moving again. He loved the role of sea captain.

"We were talking about pirates!" she told me as it came back to her.

"That's right."

"And debating a basis for right and wrong."

"Which we'll let rest for now."

She was coming fully around. She put her hand to her head. "Well, shiver me timbers."

Chapter 3

NIGHTMARE OF MURDER

The winds were steady and gentle when the *Barbee Jay* reached the island of St. Jacob and we dropped anchor in the harbor. To the west, just over a heavily jungled ridge, the lowering sun was setting the sky on fire, washing the rippled harbor and the little village of St. Marie with gold and crimson.

Brenda, Tank, Daniel, and I were on deck, all tempted to rouse Andi to see it all.

"Better let her sleep," I finally said.

As for Andi . . .

As she lay restless in the bow's V-berth, sleep became a theater of horrors as dark visions tumbled through her mind: The sea, dark and boiling; a pirate with red scarf and stubbly chin; the belly of an old ship at sea, rocking, the planks and timbers groaning; another pirate with a long black beard, laughing, the glint of gold in his mouth; the *zing!* of a cutlass being drawn; clashing blades.

Then came threatening faces emerging from the night. Cold, cruel eyes. A blond man, his face wrinkled, his hair thin. A big Asian man, all in black, wielding a knife.

"You really thought you'd get away?" said the blond man.

"This is no game," said the Asian, waving the knife blade closer, closer.

Banana Peel. The words bore no meaning, but they terrified her.

They clamped onto her with a painful, iron grip. Terror. Choking. A slap across the face like a lashing, burning fire.

She kicked violently under the blanket, writhing, trying to get free. "No . . . no! Not me!"

The visions continued . . .

"Where is the money?" they asked. "Tell us or you will bleed."

Can't remember, can't remember!

Then you will bleed. You will die.

The knife -

"NO!" She wanted to wake up but could not.

The visions coalesced into a nightmare . . .

Grappling, breaking free, she ran down shadowy, empty streets, through alleys and archways in the dark. *Can't shout, can't call for help, no one must know . . .*

Footsteps behind her. The knife blade flashing in a patch of moonlight.

A long pier with boats on either side. The hollow *clump! clump!* of the planks under her feet, the hiss of surf.

Grabbed! An iron hand on her arm! Blows to her face! Striking back, lashing, trying to get free.

Water, all around her. Stinging salt filling her mouth, her throat, her lungs.

Fire in her chest! FIRE!

With a muffled scream she kicked off her blanket and leaped from the berth, bounding about the main cabin like a pinball, banging her head on the ceiling, groping for a way out, yelling, screaming, lashing with her arms.

We collided with each other trying to get down the companionway. Brenda stopped short at the base of the steps while the rest of us piled up behind her, aghast.

Andi was like a trapped animal, crouching, fists clenched, throwing punches and kicking at enemies who weren't there. "Touch me and I'll take your hands for me trophy, by the powers!" She was still wearing her pirate costume, right down to the scarf and earring.

"Andi . . . " Brenda spoke in a hushed voice, reaching out to her.

Andi planted a mean punch to her jaw, sending her into the galley cabinets. "I'll take you all like a man, and you scurvy scum!"

Tank got close enough to see into her eyes. "She's walking in her –" Her foot in his chest sent him to the floor. "—sleep!"

I took hold of her from behind. "Andi, you're

going to hurt yourself — OOF!" Her elbow rammed into my gut and I lost my grip on her, my vision going dark.

"Nay," she said, "but *you'll* have me for shark bait if I know my own name!" She leaped upon the dining table, her rubber cutlass in her hand. "I'll be free o' you all or under the hatches, you can lay to that!"

Brenda and Daniel blocked the companionway lest Andi find her way overboard. Tank grabbed one leg, I grabbed the other, and we pulled her down as she took to us with her fists. I saw stars, but somehow I held on.

With a free hand she yanked open the cutlery drawer.

I grabbed for that hand. I missed.

She let out a yell, "Take that, Banana Peel!" and a knife sailed through the air.

Brenda ducked and the knife thudded into the paneling right behind her. A perfect throw.

We pig-piled on top of her, even Daniel, and that seemed to arrest her madness. At least, she ceased fighting.

Brenda, warily easing off the pile and shielding Daniel, called to her, "Andi? Earth to Andi, come in."

"You awake now?" Tank asked, side glancing at the knife still quivering in the wall.

Andi was alarmed to find herself on the floor. "I was having a dream. Somebody was trying to kill me, and I ran away, and then they caught me and . . . they just kept wailing on me, beating me silly 'til I fell in the water and drowned."

Tank and I exchanged a look, and slowly let her up.

The fight was over. We guided Andi to the dinette

where she sat down and, with a trembling hand, removed the scarf from her head. "I could see them. I could even smell them."

Brenda pulled the knife from the wall and placed it back in the drawer. Then she turned, arms crossed, and studied Andi. We all studied Andi, so much it made her nervous.

"I didn't ask for this."

"Like . . . heck you didn't." Apparently Brenda was trying to be gentle with her words. "Playin' pirate with all that pirate talk and that getup when you got wires loose? Yeah, you were askin' for it."

"And you could have hurt yourself," I added. "You almost hurt us."

"Almost?" Tank said, discovering blood from fingernail gouges near his eyes.

I waxed fatherly, a role I hardly expected. "The pirate show on St. Clemens captured your imagination, and we don't fault that, but it's definitely time to put this fantasy aside."

"But —"

"But nothin'!" said Brenda. "How much is enough for you? You threw a knife at me! That's enough! That's plenty!"

"But . . . " Andi actually marveled. "I didn't do that. I mean, I did it, but . . . but I didn't do it really. I don't know how to throw knives."

"You do now," said Tank.

Awkward silence.

"Tomorrow we'll go ashore and just . . . vacation," I said. "It's what Adrian Pugh and his family did anyway, and it'll give you a chance to have some solid land under your feet. And please, doff that pirate outfit. Just be my geekish assistant for a change."

Andi removed her scabbard and rubber cutlass and placed them on the counter.

Brenda put out her hand. "And how about that earring?"

Andi's hand went to her ear. "Oh! It's still there!" She smiled, relieved. "I dreamed they tore it off."

"Who tore it off?" Tank asked.

"The guys who killed me."

Brenda still had her hand out. Andi removed the earring and, with sadness, handed it over.

"Tomorrow," I said, "we're getting off this boat."

Chapter 4

A PIRATE AT BREAKFAST

The next day dawned bright and clear, a perfect day to go ashore and repeat Adrian Pugh's itinerary: snorkeling, hiking, a visit to a bird sanctuary. It seemed these benign, diversionary activities held little promise of a revelation, but at the very least they would be helpful toward reconnecting Andi's "loose wires."

When we sat at the table for breakfast Andi

remained topside, primping, we supposed. When she finally descended the companionway, it was with a flourish. "And the top o' the mornin' to ya!"

"Good morning," said Brenda and Tank.

"Good —what did you do?" I said.

As she sat at the table, she looked fairly normal in a sun suit and matching sun visor.

It was the beard and mustache she'd drawn on her lip and chin that struck us as a little odd — a thin, handlebar mustache with loops at each end, and a tight little goatee. "Am I not fit for your table now, as smart as a bright feathered cock, and trimmed for the finest company!"

Our staring seemed to perplex her. She checked herself over. "Have I overlooked something, and begging your pardon!"

"You still doin' that pirate stuff?" said Brenda.

I gave a little signal with my hand and Brenda, much to be commended, put her lecture on hold. "Andi. You've drawn a mustache and a beard on your face."

She stared at us for a moment, then looked for something that would serve as a mirror. A shiny cream pitcher served the purpose. "Well — !" She touched her chin in wonderment, and then turned red. "All right, who did it?"

We went blank, still a step behind whatever was happening.

Which only fueled her anger. "Don't give me that innocent look!"

Tank ventured, "We didn't do anything. You did it to yourself!"

I corroborated, "That artwork on your face wasn't there until you went topside to fix yourself up."

Suddenly, with a different demeanor, she set down the cream pitcher, nodded grimly, and crossed her arms. Andi the Pirate spoke again, "Aye, so *that's* the way of it. Betrayal again, and by me own shipmates. If you cannot trust your chin to your friends, now where can you leave it, tell me that!"

We looked at each other. The trouble wasn't over.

Where to begin? "Andi, I think maybe you need —"

"I'll tell you what old Ben needs!" she spouted, pointing her finger at me. "Maybe just one day, nay, one little moment, when —" She stopped, staring at her pointing hand, rubbing her third finger with her thumb, looking at it as if she'd never noticed it before. "Blimey! Me finger's back on." We were nonplussed, so she explained, "Lost it, you see. Had a mainsheet wrapped around it and I weren't aware. A good gust of wind come along, and *yank!* Off she went. Became food for fish, you can lay to that."

"You lost a finger?" I asked.

She gave me an impatient scowl. "Long you've been a mate of mine, Cap, and now you don't remember? Been touching the rum again?"

"Well . . . " I looked around the table, at every other set of eyes. "The food's getting cold."

We acted normal, passing eggs and French toast around, enjoying it as best we could, and talking about our plans for the day. Except Daniel. As Andi the Pirate stabbed her food with her knife, chewed rudely, and drooled, he couldn't take his eyes off her. He reached for his knife — and Brenda intercepted that whole notion before he could touch it.

But at some point I didn't notice, Andi resorted to her fork and wiped her drool with her napkin. "How far to that coral reef?"

Tank answered, "Just around the point, over on the west side."

"Gotta snorkel today. Can't miss it."

Andi again?

Brenda was ready for a retry. "What's that on your chin?"

Andi found the cream pitcher again and used it as a mirror. "Oh!" She laughed with embarrassment. "Sorry. I guess I got carried away this morning." She promptly went to the head - the washroom - to wash it off.

And so began a perfectly glorious day — that ended much worse.

KIDNAPPED

All day we enjoyed the pleasure of repeating the Pugh family's vacation: snorkeling, hiking to the top of the island's highest mountain, exploring the closely arranged, meandering village of St. Marie to the sound of Caribbean music. We had dinner in a family run seafood shop on the waterfront and could see the *Barbee Jay* through the front windows, rocking ever so slightly on the end of her anchor chain. Whether any of this had anything to do with the loss of millions in investors' money we did not discover.

As dusk approached and we sat on the wharf enjoying ice cream bars, Andi was still restless. "Hey, before we go back to the boat, how about walking the beach?"

The rest of us were tired, ready to call it a day. Daniel was already asleep, his head in Brenda's lap. Nevertheless, Andi was being herself, and anything that could help her remain in that condition suited me. I steeled myself against my own exhaustion and said, "I'll go with you. But we have to be back before sunset."

She jumped up. "Come on!" Before I could reach walking speed she'd run from the wharf to the sand below, sending the tiny sand crabs scurrying. True to her plan, she kicked off and carried her shoes.

I made my way along after her, staying close to the wet sand near the water for better firmness under my feet, and I left my shoes on, thank you. She slowed her pace, I caught up, and we walked together, stepping around tiny crab burrows and watching a pair of pelicans nabbing fish from the waves. Entirely therapeutic, or so I hoped.

As we rounded a point, Andi reached into her pocket, drew out her oversized, gold earring, and looped it through her ear.

"Well now," I said, "where did you get that?"

"From Brenda's stash of stuff."

Wishing to avoid any further debate on right and wrong and whether or where a basis might be found for them, I didn't question her ethics. "But of course there's a risk involved, as we've observed —"

Abruptly, she stopped in her tracks and assumed a familiar, roguish posture. "And from what tired old scow did you scrape that one? I've a right to me druthers, same's do you!"

I winced. Oh no.

She swaggered in front of me like bar scum wanting a brawl. "Learn if you can, laddie. There's no right or wrong in this world, only what a man makes for himself, you can lay to that!"

So we were into it again — whoever we were.

She turned her back on me and stomped away with a masculine gait. I followed, temper rising above discretion. "Andi — or whoever you are, I don't give a hoot in hell — that will be quite enough!"

There was a snap and a rustle in the trees beside us. I saw something stirring, most likely an animal. But a large one.

"What are you looking at?" Andi asked.

"Nothing. Now you –" As I looked at her, she was Andi again. "Andi?"

With abrupt innocence, she answered "What?"

"*Andi?*"

She replied impatiently. "*What?*"

I was stymied between three courses. What was I to be, her employer, her father, or her therapist?

She said with a wrinkled nose, "You are acting so weird."

I rubbed my forehead, admittedly to hide my eyes. "Wouldn't it be fair for me to know from moment to moment to whom I'm speaking?"

She looked around. "It's just us, Professor."

"So . . . Andi. May we talk about that earring?"

Her hand went nervously to her ear. "Okay, okay. So Brenda's gonna be ticked off at me."

"You're quite right."

"But . . . " A slight sneer curled her lip. "I been through heavier storms than what she can bring, and I'll weather this one too! Besides, didn't I tell ya there's no right or wrong in this world, no true or false, and that's the way of it?"

Since when did Andi agree with me on that subject? "Ben, I presume?"

A hushed voice came from the trees. "Aye, that's her!"

I saw no one, but someone was there. "We have company."

She pulled in close to me, crouching and wary. "Aye," she answered in a stealthy whisper. "and it's more than a creature afoot. I might know that voice."

I shot her a sideways glance. "You know who it is?"

Andi looked back at me. "Who *who* is?"

I gave up trying to talk to her. I just grabbed her hand. "We're getting out of here!"

"YAY!!!!" In a flashing moment, bursting from the jungle and hemming us in against the sea, a filthy band of hairy and sweating scoundrels with muscular arms, sashes, pistols, scarved heads, flashing cutlasses, and grinning teeth closed upon us like vultures upon carrion.

Pirates! At least a dozen. It was unreal. It was frightening.

Of course, I reminded myself, it had to be a paid prank, a bonus feature of the St. Clemens pirate show. Someone had put them up to this. I managed a good-humored smile, entirely a lie.

Andi didn't smile at all — she snarled, facing down an oversized caricature in a black leather vest and three-cornered pirate hat. "Rock, if it's a meeting the Cap wants, he coulda sent a note!"

The caricature pointed at the earring and exchanged a nod with a bare-chested monster of superfluous muscle. "Aye, that's her!"

"Let's take her!" said the monster.

The other pirates burst into laughter and closed in on us like castle walls collapsing.

Andi reached for a sword she was no longer wearing, found nothing, and looked at me, awakened.

"What's happening?"

The pirate Rock grabbed her up. Three more pirates took hold of her arms and legs while a fifth threw a blanket over her. I spun about as pirates closed in, ready to inflict injury any way I could, but it was useless. The last I saw of Andi, she was writhing and kicking, wrapped in a blanket and tied with rope, carried by two laughing pirates. That was a millisecond before a blanket swallowed me and I was helpless in a woolen cocoon and borne aloft.

I could still hear Andi's muffled screaming.

Chapter 6

THE PREDATOR

When our captors untied our bonds and lifted away the blankets, it was only because we were in a wooden boat and there was nowhere for Andi and I to run without the ability to walk on miles and miles of open water. Dead ahead, in silhouette against the reddened sky, lay our destination, a three-masted, square-rigged pirate ship right out of Robert Louis Stevenson — or the pirate show on St. Clemens. Andi, now herself and immersed in the fantasy, drank in the sight. I could only hope Tank and Brenda had arranged all this. If not, they would have no idea where we were, and worse yet, these ruffians, whatever their game, weren't kidding.

Rowing with precision, our surly hosts brought the boat alongside. Andi scurried up the rope ladder and over the bulwark with no help. I climbed well enough, motivated by my preference for a larger boat over a smaller one.

The ship smelled of oak and tar and creaked with the swells in deep, wooden tones. The rigging, stretched with a spider's precision, the masts, yards, and sails, now furled, were worthy of a tour in themselves, but we were granted no time to gawk. Still prisoners and treated as such, we were hurried along toward a door below the quarterdeck, the portal, I supposed, that led to the Captain's Quarters.

I was right. Inside, under the low beamed ceiling, sitting at a map table under lamplight, was the Captain, a steely-eyed character from another age with black curls down to his shoulders and beard to his breast. I came within an impulse of laughing, but thought better of it. He gestured with his hand and his men placed us firmly in two chairs facing him across the table.

He studied us a moment — mostly Andi — and then, of all things, began to sing what I guessed was an old sea shanty:

"Haul on the bowlin', the fore and maintop bowlin' . . . "

And to my surprise, Andi gave the musical answer:
"Haul on the bowlin', the bowlin' haul!"
The Captain rose to his feet for the next line,
"Haul on the bowlin', the packet is a-rollin' . . . "
And Andi, eyes widening at her own knowledge, sang the response,
"Haul on the bowlin', the bowlin' haul!"
The Captain cocked an eyebrow and exchanged a look with his men.

To which Andi took on a scowl that wasn't hers. "And what of it, Cap? Set your course with tremblin' or you'll stay in irons. The wind only blows when I whistle." Then she marveled and looked at me. "What did I say?"

"By the powers, it's Ben!" rumbled the monster, and the room filled with a tension I could feel.

The Captain stared at Andi's gold earring, and then at her. "So, might you tell me where you are?"

She answered as if she'd known it all her life. "Aboard the *Predator*." She gasped, stunned. She looked around the room at the costumed cutthroats, and I saw recognition in her eyes.

So did the Captain. "So you been here before, lass. You know these faces."

Of course, she had to have seen some of these thugs as characters in the pirate show, but we never heard their names. Even so . . .

She looked up at the oversized caricature in leather vest and three-cornered pirate hat. "Rock."

Rock snorted a chuckle and nodded.

"And . . . " She recognized the muscular monster. "Scalarag."

He gave a mocking bow. "M'lady!"

She stared, then pointed at the ship's token bald guy, the one with the bushy mustache and oversized saber. "Norwig . . . the Bean!"

Norwig cocked an equally bushy eyebrow and looked at the Captain.

She named the other three: the mousy little raisin was Spikenose — he served as the ship's purser and cook; the morose man with the scar across his face was, naturally, Harry the Scar; the flamboyant, Doug Fairbanks throwback was Jean-Pierre DuBois.

As for the Captain: "And you're . . . Captain Thatch." She looked at me. "How . . . how did I do that?"

As if I had an answer. "I'm sure we'd all like to know."

"You bought that earring," said the Captain. "We were missing it, and there was talk around St. Clemens about you. The rest we tried guessing, and we guessed right." The Captain extended his hand. "I'll take that earring now."

She shied back.

"Let him have it!" I advised, touching her shoulder to steady her.

She removed it from her ear and handed it over.

He smiled, a glint of gold in his teeth, and touched a button on an incongruous intercom. "We have it. We'll see if it talks." He tried putting the earring on his own ear but only grew impatient. "Here," he said, handing it to DuBois. "You and Sparks make an inquiry."

DuBois hurried out the door.

The Captain gestured to Rock, who produced a three-cornered hat from a cabinet. "You want to be a pirate, lass, you need to look the part," said Rock. "See how this suits you." He placed it on her head.

A little big. She started to take it off —

The Captain cautioned her with a wiggle of his finger to keep it on.

There followed an odd space of time, a silence as if we were all waiting for something.

It finally came, though clearly unexpected: the horrible scream of a soul in hell from somewhere in the hull of the ship. It made us all start. The sounds of a commotion followed: shouts, poundings, more screaming. I could plainly read fear and consternation in the eyes of the men as they looked to the Captain.

An electronic warble sounded from the Captain's

desk. He reached, pressed a button on the intercom. "Yes?"

"Captain!" came a voice, "you'd better get down here!"

With a muffled curse, the Captain dashed out of the room. Through the door he left open we could see him dropping through the companion to the decks below.

I eyed the intercom. "Interesting device you have there . . . for the seventeenth century."

Any attempt at levity was lost on these men. They responded by tightening their circle around Andi and me, fingering their knives, swords, pistols.

We could hear no small row between the Captain and someone else down below. That someone would soon be walking the plank, it seemed . . . or keel-hauled, or flogged, or hung from the yardarm . . . or given a pink slip and a severance package, depending on the century.

The next thing we heard was the Captain's boots thundering on the deck below and up the wooden stairs of the companion. He crossed the deck like an approaching thunderstorm, burst through the cabin doorway, and went directly to Andi, snatching the hat from her head and dashing it to the floor. "Seems it doesn't become you!"

Another volley of screams, this time muffled by a few more bulkheads, found it's way through the door.

"Close that door!" the Captain hollered.

Spikenose slammed it shut.

The Captain fumed, paced, looked at his men, looked at us, and finally, with only slight control of his temper, told Andi, "Lassie, it looks like you and your father are going to be with us a while!"

"Uh, well, I'm not –" I stopped. At this moment, what could be less important? Instead, "If I may ask, just what do you want with us? I don't understand any of this, if you don't mind my saying."

The Captain sat on the edge of the table and took a dagger from his belt. He played with it, stabbing it into the table and giving it a wicked twist. "Memory, Mr. . . . ."

"McKinney. James McKinney, PhD."

He looked at Andi.

"Andrea Goldstein, assistant to Professor McKinney," she said.

The Captain looked down the blade of his dagger as he continued to auger its tip into the tabletop. "Well, it matters little now who you are. What matters is what the lass remembers, and you'll be staying here, looking around, seeing our faces and seeing our ship until she does remember."

"Remember what?" I asked.

He gave the dagger a flip and caught it again by its handle. "Everything."

Chapter 7

THE TECHNO-LAIR

By the time Tank, Brenda, and Daniel grew concerned, borrowed flashlights from the seafood restaurant, and found the site of our abduction, the darkness had closed in and the tide would soon follow. Hurriedly, they examined the signs left in the sand even as the waves were steadily licking them up.

Brenda tried to count the different prints. "Man, I dunno . . . looks like six, maybe."

"This might be number seven," said Tank, pointing with his light. "Looks a bit smaller. It's got a different tread, you see that?"

"I see enough. We're in deep" —she noticed young Daniel nearby —"poop. Whatever we were lookin' for, it found us."

"So why'd they only grab Andi and the professor?"

Brenda shined her light in a nervous circle. "Who

says they aren't after us too? Daniel! Stay close!"

There was a clear trail of tracks leading from, and back into the jungle.

"Hoo boy . . . " said Tank.

Brenda used the word she avoided the last time and they all went together, crossing the sand and stepping into the trees and the tangle, ducking under limbs, pushing aside vines. The dark under the jungle canopy was nearly total.

It was just as they began to question the wisdom of this exploration that they emerged on the other side of what was a narrow isthmus and found themselves on another beach.

Now Daniel, like a hound catching a scent, hurried over the sand, tracing the tracks toward the surf. Brenda kept her light on Daniel as they ran after; Tank beamed his light up and down the beach, knowing they were wide open and vulnerable.

"Tank!" Brenda called. "He's on it! He's found it!"

They hurried to where the child had halted, and there, in the beam of their lights, was a clear groove in the sand formed by the keel of a boat that was once there, but now was gone. Their lights would only reach so far over the surf, lighting up the closest waves breaking, and beyond that, nothing.

* * *

In a way, we got our tour of the Predator. With Captain Thatch, Rock, and Scalarag as tour guides — to put it kindly —we walked the upper decks by the light of carried lamps and learned the locations and names of the forecastle, poop deck, and quarterdeck, the functions of the foremast, main mast, and mizzen mast, and the sails affixed to each mast with their respective yards, the main, top, and topgallant. All of this was unavoidably interesting, but Captain Thatch's main interest was Andi and what, by whatever means, she knew.

Which was a lot. She could already tell Thatch the names of the decks, the masts, the blocks and rigging. She could name the cannons by the size of the balls they fired: 12, 24, and 68 pounders. She blithely referred to the 68 pounders by their nickname, "smashers," and when Thatch said the orlop deck was our next stop, she knew how to get there, leading the way down the companion steps, through several decks, and to the deck immediately above the hold, a dark, low-ceilinged space below the ship's waterline.

There, moving along a narrow corridor, she recognized a cabin, no bigger than absolutely necessary, in which there was a narrow cot, a minuscule desk, and an empty closet the size of a cupboard. She lingered at the door, inquisitive, but by now Thatch was so impressed by her performance that he hurried us along to another tight little space between bulkheads and decks.

Well. After all the touring in the seventeenth century, this room was a jarring change. It was lined and filled with 21st century gadgetry: computers, monitors, servers, banks of electronic gear with a dazzling array of blinking numbers and lights. Seated before it all was a half-pirate, I would say. He wore a striped shirt, red headscarf, and even a gold earring, but he was wearing Levis and canvas running shoes.

"This is Sparks," said Captain Thatch.

Sparks offered his hand —he was the first one on this ship to do so. I shook his hand, as did Andi.

"So now we're back in the real world," I quipped.

That was ill-timed. The Captain grabbed a handful

of my shirtfront and growled in my face, "It's all real, old man, as real as this fist under your chin! Out here, we have it our way, and our way is where you are." He cocked an eyebrow at me, expecting acknowledgement.

"You're the Captain," I replied, convinced this man was no stranger to brute force.

Then, as if to heighten the tension, the same maniacal scream we'd heard before came through the boards below our feet, all the more terrifying for its proximity. We couldn't ignore it. With my eyes I questioned the Captain.

"Pay it no mind," he said even as he glared at Sparks. "It isn't really there."

I was in no place to argue, but it did seem to bother him well enough.

Just as it bothered Sparks. He was clearly troubled by the scream and pled with the Captain, "I can fix it. I just need some time to figure out Ben's programming."

Captain Thatch was more interested in watching Andi. "Look around you, Lass. Seen it before?"

Andi's eyes were already locked on the computer screen, on the rows of numbers and code that I found undecipherable. "It looks so familiar!"

"Have a seat," said Thatch, nudging Sparks from his chair and offering it to Andi.

She sat before the monitor and studied it, hands on the keyboard, scrolling down, up again, looking surprised as if she knew what she was looking at. "Well . . . no wonder!"

The Captain leaned in close, examining the monitor along with her. "Yes, my dear? What do you see?"

"The system is scrambled. It's . . . " She scrolled up and down, pointing at lines of code. "See here? It's an encrypted command in the program that engages if anyone violates the entry protocol. Instead of a sequential Brain Wave Authentication, the program inverts to Brain Wave Generation and then loops back on itself and self-scrambles. Which means . . . " She shuddered at a new awareness. "The particular Writer, W-902, would have Authenticated the wearer's brain, but then would have reloaded every brain pattern in cumulative layers of confusion. Pure madness!"

The Captain took a gold earring - Andi's gold earring - from a hook on the wall, put on his reading glasses, and read a number from the earring's inner surface. "W-902." He cursed and railed at Sparks, "And you didn't notice? You didn't say a word before he put this on?" I caught him shooting a glance toward the hold below us.

"How was I to know Ben would scramble the system? How could anybody know?"

"Eh, he's done that and more, now hasn't he? Made sure we couldn't track him, but made sure the whole system was useless without him. A little insurance, I'll wager."

"But a lot of good it did him."

"And us! Instead of information we get a scrambled brain! And what about this Thursday with the big fish to catch?"

Sparks stared at the screen, wagging his head.

Thatch was getting dangerous. "I asked you a question!"

"I don't know!"

Andi piped in, "You need the entry code." She

tapped some keys and a prompt appeared on the screen, blinking, waiting.

That got their attention. They halted their squabble and stared over her shoulder.

"Let's see . . . " she said, tapping the keys. "How about, 'Aardvark, Basil, Crustacean, 233 997 417709'?"

The computer beeped, the screen went wild, lights came on, drives whirred to life, and a very attractive lady pirate appeared on the screen, presenting a menu of links and sub-pages.

Sparks was stunned. "We're in! We're operational!"

"Almost there," said the Captain. "Well done, lass! Well done!"

The way these men whooped and high-fived each other, you'd think all wars had ceased for now and forever. Did this give us any bargaining leverage, I wondered. "I take it you're pleased?"

"Break out some grog," said the Captain to Rock, "and let's have our dinner." He looked at me and Andi, and even patted Andi on the shoulder. "And two more places for our special guests!"

Well, we seemed to be on their good side, something I hoped to use to our advantage. Andi ventured a quick look at me, and with a similar look I agreed with her: Whatever else we didn't yet know, we could be sure we'd stumbled upon the very thing we'd been sent to find. We were right in the middle of it.

Chapter 8

PRISONERS

Brenda, Tank, and Daniel soon found that St. Jacob was not a good place for their friends to be kidnapped. There was no 911 system; there wasn't even cell service. The police station was a tight little cube of concrete block with a dented Volkswagen beetle for a squad car, and no one was there. They finally found the local police chief in his squat little abode next door. Tank and Brenda spilled their story in urgent fashion as he listened, absentmindedly wiping his mouth.

"So," Tank said, "we need help, we need cops and marshals and SWAT teams and stuff."

He weighed everything a moment and then invited them in. "You need to file a complaint."

He took a blank sheet of paper, took down all the pertinent information, then added his phone number. Having completed this single page to his satisfaction, he took a fresh piece of paper and began scribbling out a copy of the first.

"What are you doin', man?" Brenda asked.

He answered matter-of-factly, "I have to make posters to spread around."

"You don't have a copy machine?" Tank asked, looking around the room.

"Do I look like I'd have a copy machine?"

Brenda was flustered, to put it mildly. "Come on, there's got to be a better way than that!"

He finished making his first copy and began copying again. "You might try the TV station."

"You have a *TV station*?"

The police chief looked insulted. "Yeah. Channel Five. Sometimes the other islands can pick up the signal, depending on the wind."

"That'll work!" said Tank.

"If you throw in some advertising."

"*What?*" said Brenda.

He motioned for calm. "Hey, no sweat. Margarita's owns the station. Cut a deal."

* * *

Andi and I had had our dinner shortly before being kidnapped, but under the circumstances we determined to enjoy our "hosts'" hospitality and joined Captain Thatch, Sparks, Rock, and Scalarag for dinner in the Captain's quarters. We ate and raved about the beef, garlic potatoes, and broccoli, and even managed to squeeze down a solvent of some kind called grog, all to keep things warm and human.

The conversation trended toward the pirate life in a modern world, and so I asked offhandedly, "So it seems you've chosen a seventeenth century reality over a modern one?"

Captain Thatch took a gulp of grog and replied, "Why not? Who's to say what's true but what there is on the *Predator*? No right, no wrong, no present, no past, just what is, and how we like it."

I gave Andi a side glance. "We were on this very subject not long ago, Andi and I."

"Of a certain. It's the talk these days. No Truth, no Shame, no God to draw the line."

I glanced at Andi again. "Yes, that is, after all, what it comes down to, and so here you are."

"And so here *you* are. Can't say we've done you wrong, now can we?"

Now Andi shot *me* a glance.

"Well . . . " I could hardly agree, but as Andi's eyes were telling me, what reason could I provide for disagreement? "That could depend on the recipient of the action, I suppose, whether the action would be in their best interests."

The Captain laughed. "Their best interests? So now you've come up with a rule." Then he looked at me craftily, like the spider at the fly. "But them that makes the rules, has their own interests, you can lay to that." He nodded toward Andi. "Like the pretty lass you have here, old man. Some real opportunity, I'd say, when it's you that pays her."

I hoped he was only pressing a point. "That would be unthinkable, of course."

"Unthinkable? *I* thought of it." He gestured with his fork. "So I'll wager so have you."

"If I were one to violate trust and honor!"

"Ha! Honor! Hardly a useful sentiment!"

"Quite useful in holding a ship together, I would think!" I recalled a quote from C.S. Lewis. "'We laugh at honor and are shocked to find traitors in our midst.'"

He scoffed at that, so of course I had to challenge him, and while we bickered over where such things as honor could come from and whether they existed outside of human choice and how they could be found in the absence of God— which was a moot point because, I argued, there was no God — I noticed Andi picking up a banana and peeling it, gawking at it as if seeing a vision, oblivious to the debate.

"If there be no trust and no honor," said the Captain, watching Andi, "then there be left only the animal we are–Am I right, Ben?"

Andi snapped out of her preoccupation and answered without pause, "Aye, Captain!"

The Captain laughed and slapped the table in victory as his crewmen marveled. Andi was surprised, and then, I think, afraid for herself.

"So we're talking truth, are we?" said the Captain, peering over the table at her as he spoke to me. "Well, for your truth you have a lovely assistant with joys to offer, but for my truth . . . " He pointed with his fork. "I think I might be talking to an old friend of mine." He addressed Andi."Ben? You're looking a lot prettier these days!"

Andi shrank into her chair.

Sparks eyed her as if she were one of his

41

computers. "The system's back online. We could try another download."

Thatch had to think about that.

"We'll just check for a signal, that's all," said Sparks.

Finally, the Captain nodded. "Fair enough."

Rock produced the same hat they'd placed on her head before, and placed it on her head again as Sparks went out the door and then below decks.

The same eerie space of time passed– last time, it ended with a scream. I was afraid for Andi, angry with myself. Just when I thought Captain Thatch and I were, well, compatriots in opinion, I found I'd been foolishly letting him play a game with me, and now what would become of Andi?

The intercom warbled as before and the Captain answered, "Well?"

"Nothing, Captain," came Sparks' voice over the speaker. "We can only load firsthand memory, not secondhand."

Thatch roared and pounded the table, his face contorted with a bestial anger I'd not yet seen. He bolted around the table, his hands going for Andi's neck. I reacted without hesitation, but had come only an inch out of my chair when Rock and Scalarag shoved me down with all their weight and held me there.

The Captain's hands trembled around Andi's neck as if he longed to wring it but dared not. "You're . . . you're in there, aren't you? Hiding from an old friend. A *friend*!" He turned away, so angry he couldn't choose how to conduct himself –surely it was not with any dignity. "You turned on me, didn't you?" He turned and faced her again. "You sold me out!"

Andi was at a total loss. "Sir, I don't know what you're talking about!" She broke into tears. "I don't know what's happening to me!"

He took a moment to contain himself, then smirked at her. "Well I do, lass, I do, so we'll be keeping you a while." He let his cold, angry gaze dart between the two of us. "And give no mind to leaving the ship. Try to escape, and we'll sever the tendons behind your knees, roll you up in squid guts, and throw you to the sharks!" He looked at me as if looks could spit and ordered Rock and Scalarag, "Put this man in irons! Perhaps the lass will act in his . . . best interests!"

Chapter 9

THE SEARCH BEGINS

Margarita's, favored drinking establishment of St. Jacobs, opened its doors at ten the next morning. The police chief, wielding a palm-sized handycam, waved Tank and Brenda to their marks on the beachside veranda, got some drinks in their hands —a Margarita for Brenda, a grapefruit juice for Tank —and coached the customers to yuk it up in the background. "Okay, rolling."

As a TV personality, Tank was, well, a good athlete. He didn't know what else in the world to do than stare a hole through the camera. "Hi, I'm Tank."

Brenda, in fruit basket hat and flowered halter top, blossomed as the finest of Caribbean beach bimbos, wielding her drink and swiveling her shoulders. "Hey, mon! I'm Brennnda! You lika me? I lika you! We got friends, you know?" She held up drawings she'd made of myself and Andi — quite good, actually. "They are missing. Gone poof! You help us find them, no? They were on St. Jacobs just last night, but where they are now, nobody knows! You know? You call us here at . . . " She gave a grand, airheaded flourish! "MARGARITA'S! The happiest place on St. Jacobs!"

"Yeah," said Tank.

"Dos Equis on tap, Happy Hour at four!"

"Yeah," said Tank.

"And . . . " said the police chief, "cut!"

And . . . Brenda tossed the fruit basket hat on a table and shook out her dreadlocks. "Okay, cool, we're on TV and the cops are in the loop. Now let's get workin'."

Daniel, being a minor, was waiting outside.

He was wearing a Margarita's pirate hat. Brenda was about to ask –

"Part of the deal," said the lady proprietor. "Cute kid."

Daniel held the hat on his head and met their eyes like it was something important. Brenda got it. "Pirates," she said. "It's got something to do with pirates. Andi had pirates on the brain."

Tank nodded, reading Daniel's eyes. "Ever since that pirate show on St. Clemens."

They came to the same conclusion: "We've got to get back there!"

But in the *Barbee Jay*? A sailboat was so slow, and they were novices at sailing.

"Hey, mon," came a voice. "Need a lift to St. Clemens?"

A jovial looking fellow stood on the dock below Margarita's. He was . . . Jamaican? Native? Hispanic? Under that straw hat and behind that mustache he bore a remarkable resemblance to a cabby they'd met in Rome and another cabby Brenda had met in Florida, and those other guys had the same gift for showing up at just the right moment. This guy had one foot on the dock and the other on a speedboat with not one, but two oversized outboards.

"How much?" Tank asked.

And there was that same grin they'd seen before. "Part of the deal."

* * *

The ship did have leg irons bolted to the main mast where the recalcitrant could be bound in the sight of all, but a man so shackled would be unfit for swabbing the deck and so, free of chains and mop in hand, I labored under watchful eyes. Rock, perched on the forecastle and holding a crude leather flail, supervised. Norwig the Bean hauled up buckets of seawater to rinse.

"Move along, old man!" Rock hollered. "And work as fit as the young or feel the lash!"

I worked with "youthful" vigor while Norwig kept the deck awash before my mop. We were getting results —until the little raisin Spikenose came up from the galley with a pail of kitchen waste and faked a stumble, spilling the sour contents where I had just cleaned.

"Oops," he said, then turned and left.

"Ya scum!" Rock hollered at me. "Is that what you call a clean deck?" He hopped down, scooped up a sizable handful of fats and fruit peelings and hurled them at me. I could have ducked, I suppose, but that wasn't the object, was it? They were out to humiliate me and I thought it best to let them.

"What's that slop on the front of you?" asked Norwig as he promptly doused me with a bucket of seawater.

They laughed. Of course.

Temper, McKinney, I thought as I felt my face burn. *Master your temper!*

"Behold the man of great words!" Rock shouted, then looked at me with disdain. "But you can't talk the dirt off this deck, now can you? On this ship it's not words but work, and a man holds his own if he's a man."

"Aye, sir!" I replied, and with a bit of show I mopped the foul residue from the deck as Norwig splashed it along the bulwark and over the side.

Rock nodded, the mollified taskmaster. "So what were you back home, old man?"

He asked me in past tense, and so I answered from the past. "A priest."

His eyes grew wide—mockingly.

Before I saw it coming, a blow from his flail landed on the side of my face. I don't remember hitting the deck I'd just cleaned; I was too stunned to feel it.

I do remember him standing over me, flail in hand, delighted at the wretch he'd made of me. "So let's see you turn the other cheek!"

* * *

I was fearful for Andi, as she was for me, but we'd set our strategy with eye contact, expressions, planted phrases: we must cooperate, try to please, get things "human," and hopefully draw any information we could from our captors.

So, while I was up on deck getting humiliated and clobbered, she was in the cabin she'd seen earlier, desperate to recall anything the Captain might find useful, trying to be of value. He was, after all, alone with her down here, and as he'd said, there was no truth or shame, no God aboard this ship to draw the line.

"This is Ben's cabin, isn't it?" she asked.

"That it is," said the Captain. "Or, was."

She nodded. "My–*his* things are gone. He used to have a big case right there in that corner with all his documentation."

He placed his hand under her chin and turned her face toward him. "Ben. What were your plans?"

"By the powers, Cap–" She shook away the lingo that kept cropping up in her head and spoke for herself. "I, he, had to get off this ship. He had to get free and on his own before anything happened."

"What . . . anything?"

The words–and the terror–popped into her mind. "Ere we all get killed, and it be no wives' tale. As sure as I know m'name, they'll cut us and gut us and call it a pleasure!"

Chapter 10

TWO DEAD MEN

Dr. Eli Torres was a General Practitioner on St. Clemens, but it was his side job as St. Clemens' Medical Examiner that brought a powerful athlete, a black urban female, and a ten-year-old child to the waiting room of his small practice. "A . . . drowning victim?"

"That's right, sir," said Tank. "We went by the pirate show to check around, but they're closed because a member of the cast died in a drowning accident. We figured you'd know something about that."

Dr. Torres eyed the motley trio on the other side of the counter and wagged his head. "I really can't talk about it."

"Well," said Brenda, "could you just answer us this: Did the victim have a tight little goatee and a curly mustache? Was his left earlobe torn from an earring being torn out? Was he missing the third finger of his right hand and was he beat up before he drowned?"

With a furtive look around the waiting room–it was empty at the moment so no one else saw them– Dr. Torres asked his receptionist, "What's our next appointment?"

She checked. "Well, it's–"

"Cancel it."

The doctor swung the clinic door open and urged them through. He led them into his office and closed the door. "Now. Start from the beginning."

"Pirates!" said Daniel, still wearing the pirate hat.

Dr. Torres looked at Brenda and Tank for confirmation.

Tank just said it. "Our two friends were kidnapped on St. Jacobs, and we think it was by pirates, and so . . . we're looking for pirates."

Brenda jumped in. "Especially the one I described to you . . . I think." She was exasperated. "This is going to take a lot of explaining –"

Torres raised a hand to call a halt and said, "Have you been to the police?"

"Yeah," said Tank. "On St. Jacobs."

"And here too," said Brenda.

Torres smiled. "And that's why you've come to me on your own."

"The cops are kinda slow," Tank admitted.

"We were hoping they'd jump all over this," said Brenda.

"No, this they're not jumping on," said Torres. "I suppose they told you, one was an accident and the other was a suicide?"

"No," said Brenda, "they didn't tell us much of anything, they just –Uh . . . what? The *other?*"

"Two drownings, back to back. I've got them both in the cooler right now, in there with some frozen fruit and a marlin. The first one's the victim you described. The other one's a shopkeeper who drowned soon after."

"A shopkeeper?" said Tank. "You mean, a guy who runs a little tourist store?"

"Like along the waterfront near the cruise ships?" Brenda asked.

Torres filled in, "Like the Catch as Catch Can Emporium?" Their wide-eyed reaction must have confirmed something for him. "So you know something about that too." He took a moment, leaning back in his chair. "All right. Time out. Take a breath."

They took a breath, maybe several.

Dr. Torres lowered his voice. "I like living here. I like my job. I like getting up in the morning knowing I'll live through the day and my family will be safe. If . . . some family members . . . want to help identify the victims, that's fine, that's part of my job, but whatever it is you know, and whatever you figure out from this moment onward, it's your business, not mine, and I don't know anything about it. You never came to see me and after today, I never want to see you again, and I sure don't want to be seen with you, anywhere, any time. Are we clear on that?"

They nodded.

He sighed. "Maybe this will buy me a little favor

with God." He went to the door. "I have them in the back. The police didn't want them in the morgue; there'd be too many questions."

* * *

Brenda had Daniel sit in the waiting room with a child's book of animal adventures. She wasn't sure she'd be able to handle this herself.

When Dr. Torres rolled out the first victim and lifted away the sheet, she actually let out a cry, her hand over her mouth.

Tank said nothing. He just turned white and grabbed the edge of the table to steady himself.

"Ben Cardiff," said Dr. Torres. "He was a character in the pirate show. His Captain came in and identified him the day after he drowned."

The dead man's face and body were pale, waxy-looking. The eyelids were only half closed, the eyeballs beneath dead and dry.

He had a tight little goatee and a mustache with curls on the end. His right earlobe was torn loose as if someone had yanked off an earring. The third finger of his right hand was missing.

"So . . . " Tank asked, voice weak. "How did he die really?"

"Really?" said Dr. Torres. "By drowning, yes, but as you can see from the bruises and cuts, he was severely beaten first. Beaten, then he either fell or was thrown off a pier. It was no accident–but I didn't tell you that."

Brenda drew near Tank because she just needed to. She didn't have to say anything; she knew he was having the same dreadful experience of seeing a face Andi had mimicked the other morning at breakfast. "And when did he drown?"

"Last Sunday night. And . . . " The second body was standing, wrapped like a mummy next to the marlin. Dr. Torres wheeled it out with a hand truck and uncovered the face. "Neville Moore, proprietor of the Catch as Catch Can Emporium."

Brenda and Tank cringed. Being drowned, left in the water a while, and then frozen had degraded Moore's appearance from the jovial fellow they'd met on Sunday morning, right before they left St. Clemens for St. Jacob. Nevertheless, they could identify him.

"Yeah," said Tank. "We were in his store Sunday morning. He sold Andi that —"

"I don't want to know," said Torres. "I'm only letting *you* know."

"When did he die?" Brenda asked.

"Monday morning. The police told me it was a suicide — which it is *my* job to determine, but they let me know what my findings were to be." He put Moore's body back in the cooler, then Ben Cardiff's. "You'll be interested to know that Neville Moore was stabbed through the heart with surgical precision and already dead before he was thrown in the water. Which, I hope, gives you fair warning that you do not have friends here on St. Clemens. Some other parties with tremendous influence got here first." He met their eyes. "You follow?"

Chapter 11

THE RULE OF FORCE

Having swabbed the whole deck from stem to stern, my next assignment was as kitchen boy under the authority of Spikenose. Though I expected far worse, the galley was clean, modern, well appointed, and Spikenose, when separate from the others, was easy enough to work with.

"The Captain wants his afternoon tea," he said, setting out a tray with a silver tea service, quite nice for a pirate ship — I noticed it was tea for two. "Take this up to him. One quiet knock on the door, then enter, set the tray on the map table, cream and sugar on the Captain's right."

I took hold of the tray handles, but having noticed

the modern timbre of his speech, queried him with my eyes.

He caught my look, and as he dried a pan with a towel, replied in Pirate, "Aye, it's who's where on the ratlines, and Cap, he's the one at the top. I be the one slung near the bottom, and you, you're a barnacle on the keel." He smiled as if sharing a secret and spoke like a man from my century, "Sorry about the mess up there. Orders from Rock. It's how we test a man, how he finds his place. Keep it in mind and be ready. There's no virtue on this ship, only muscle." He pointed to the tray. "Now away with ya, lad, or I'll add your nose to m'puddin'!"

* * *

I knocked once, quietly, then stole into the Captain's cabin. Andi was there, seated across the table from the Captain. Their conversation ceased abruptly upon my entrance. Thatch glowered at me. I delivered the tray according to Spikenose' instructions, noting in the process the cabinet from which Rock had produced the three-cornered hat the Captain had made Andi wear. The cabinet door was open, and inside, on shelves and hooks, was a large and varied collection of hats, scarves, and earrings. Pirate accessories, one would think, but by now I knew they were more than that.

A theory confirmed, I believe, as the Captain picked up his conversation with Andi, perhaps in defiance of my being there. "Ben, did you know you're dead?"

Andi was perplexed, being very much alive.

The Captain poured her a cup of tea but his tone was not cordial. "I saw you stiff and cold, you know. Went to the doc's office and there you were, like a side of meat. And someone tore the earring right out of your ear." He set the cup of tea before her and glowered at me again, my cue to back away respectfully and get out. "You remember that earring, don't you?"

Her hand went to her mouth. Something was coming back.

Thatch leaned over the table. "That earring belonged to me!"

Even as I was backing through the door, the memory struck her violently. She put her hand over her ear and let out a yelp of pain and terror.

* * *

"An earring?" Lacey, the young shop assistant at Catch as Catch Can Emporium, spoke to Tank and Brenda through the barely cracked front door.

"Yeah," said Tank. He indicated about a three inch diameter with his thumb and index. "About that big around."

"You remember us?" asked Brenda. "We were in here Sunday morning. There was a red-haired girl with us and a stodgy old professor, remember them?"

"Uh, well, sure," the girl said.

"And Andi —that's the red-haired girl — bought the earring, remember?" asked Tank.

"No. No, I'm sorry, I don't remember anything about that. Look, we're closed."

Brenda shot a glance at the store hours: nine to nine. It was five twenty. "Very sorry for your loss, of course."

"You have to leave."

"Well, may we leave you a phone number?" She dug in her jeans pocket for a scrap of paper and scribbled down her cell number and Tank's. She passed it to Lacey through the narrow opening. "Excuse the doodles on the back. But these are our numbers if you want to talk at all."

The girl took the crinkled paper. "Okay."

"Let's eat," said Daniel.

Brenda asked Lacey, "Know of a good place to eat around here?"

"The Conch," she replied. "Great seafood." She stuck her hand out through the door just far enough to point the direction.

Brenda, Tank, and Daniel walked away, mingling with the tourists and island folk who crammed the narrow street.

"She's scared," said Brenda.

* * *

Spikenose' warning was none too soon.

Preparations for the evening meal produced the usual food scraps, and the mousy little chef piled them into the same bucket he'd spilled earlier, handing it to me to dump over the side. I never made it to the railing. The moment I emerged from the companion and onto the deck, a hairy leg jutted out to trip me. I stumbled and reeled along the deck even as a boot planted a blow to the bucket to knock it from my hands.

By some miracle, I recovered, neither falling nor letting go of the bucket, though some of the contents escaped and splattered on the boards.

Rock, Scalarag, and Norwig the Bean had been lying in wait just outside the companion, and now were having a good old laugh at my expense. Scalarag came at me, his eyes on the bucket, and . . .

What happened next would haunt me. Was it that leering face? The desperation of a prisoner with no alternatives? Within me, something *animal* overpowered reason and, with reckless power, I swung the bucket in a violent arc and struck the huge man in the face. The kitchen scraps splashed on him, on the deck, on everything; he reeled, hand to his face, and fell back against the capstan, blood trickling from his nose.

Rock and Norwig became stunned onlookers, suspended in time. Scalarag was quickly recovering, planting his feet, powering up his muscles, preparing for murder.

As for me, I considered myself as good as dead, and upon that conclusion, saw no point in timidity. I held the bucket out as if it were a weapon and said, "A word!"

Rock and Norwig looked at each other, amused.

"A *word*, says he!" said Rock.

"Aye," said Norwig, "more words. Be still me tremblin' 'art!"

And then I amazed — or rather, dismayed — myself. "If it be flesh yer hungerin' or blood yer thirstin', then step in, the lot o' ya, and be measured against me dyin' carcass, but you can lay to this: for every piece of me you take, be it nose or ear, I'll take for meself a piece a' you, so count it up and decide!"

There. Me dyin' words. Or so I thought.

Rock was the first to start laughing. Norwig came next and then, wiping the blood from his face with the back of his arm, Scalarag smiled and laughed with delight.

"So there be a man before us!" said Rock, exchanging a gleeful look with the others.

"Ask me," said Scalarag, regarding the blood smeared on his arm.

"Give the man his badge," said Rock.

Scalarag took the red scarf from his head and approached me.

I tensed. What was this, a trick? A ruse? Hidden gadgetry?

Scalarag smiled, and the smile looked friendly. "Heave to, my man. It's only a scarf."

He stepped around behind me, and tied the scarf about my head as Rock and Norwig raised their fists in the air and cheered.

Scalarag came around and clapped me on the shoulders. "You're one of us now!"

* * *

I returned to the galley with emptied bucket in hand and a pirate's scarf upon my head. Spikenose noticed the scarf, of course, but only raised a knowledgable eyebrow and went about his work.

I went back to peeling potatoes, my head a thicket of quandaries.

I was alive, and the muscular monster Scalarag was the only one injured. Astounding.

Nevertheless . . .

I had fallen to the level of an animal, yielded to temper, lashed out, abandoned reason for violence.

Nevertheless . . .

There could only be advantage in being "one of them:" perhaps safety, perhaps information.

Nevertheless . . .

I, a savage? A barbarian? Even though I could not argue against the ship's philosophy–No Truth, no Shame, no God to draw the line–I was ashamed.

Chapter 12

A NARROW ESCAPE

The Conch was a nice place — three stars, perhaps; they even had a walk-around combo playing steel drums, bass and guitar — and Daniel was just discovering that he liked calamari without encouragement from Brenda who didn't. Tank went for the mahi mahi because it sounded sophisticated, the polar opposite of hamburger. Brenda ordered sea bass.

"Pardon me," said a waitress. "Would you be Mr. and Mrs. Christiansen?"

Brenda was nearly insulted. "Whoa! I wouldn't say

that, girl."

"I'm, uh, Mr. Christiansen," said Tank.

The waitress spoke to Tank. "You have a phone call from someone named Lacey?"

Brenda and Tank exchanged a look. Brenda checked her cell phone. It was turned on.

"Uh . . . " said Tank, checking his own cell, "sure . . ."

"The phone's in the kitchen."

Brenda, Tank, and Daniel followed the waitress through the restaurant and into the kitchen where she handed them a cell phone and left them alone.

Tank looked at the cell phone curiously. He put it to his ear. "Hello?"

"Hello?" came a female voice. "This is Lacey. Is this Mr. Christiansen? Tank?" With the chefs and kitchen staff cooking and clattering, it was hard to hear.

"Yeah."

"Sorry to call you on another cell phone. I'm just afraid of hackers, you know?"

"Uh, yeah. Okay." Tank wanted to put the phone on speaker but he wasn't familiar with this make and couldn't figure out how. He held it just a little away from his ear so Brenda could lean close and listen. "Go ahead. Brenda's here too."

"And Daniel?"

"Yeah, he's here."

"Please keep him close. I'm afraid for you."

Daniel was across the room, looking out the back window. Brenda signaled and said, "Daniel, get away from the window."

Daniel looked at her in alarm and pointed toward the street.

Linked at the ears with the cell phone between, Brenda and Tank moved through the kitchen hubbub and toward the window.

"Hello?" came Lacey's voice. "You still there?"

"Yeah, yeah," said Tank as he and Brenda looked wherever Daniel was pointing. "Go ahead."

"I need to tell you that . . . " Now there was traffic noise. They couldn't make out what she said.

"Uh, say again?"

Daniel was pointing to a woman hurrying away from the restaurant with a cell phone to her ear.

"I was saying that you could be in real danger. There's a . . . " More traffic noise, a loud truck.

At that moment, an old truck passed right by the lady hurrying away. She glanced sideways.

The waitress.

"Lacey!" said Daniel.

"Honey, that's not Lacey!" said Brenda as if seeing an omen.

"No," Daniel insisted, pointing toward a side alley, "*Lacey!*"

Tank and Brenda followed Daniel's pointing finger down a side alley, and there, running frantically their direction, was Lacey — not on a cell phone. She caught sight of them through the window and gestured with flailing arms, screaming something.

"It looks like . . . *get down, giddy up* . . . " said Tank.

Suddenly a lady burst into the kitchen shouting, "Get out! Everybody out, NOW!"

Daniel started tugging at them. "Get out!"

Tank got the concept. "Get out!" he yelled.

Brenda, Tank, Daniel, the kitchen staff, the lady, all got out, scattering, finding cover. Daniel tugged Brenda and Tank into the alley, around and behind a big dumpster. Lacey, huffing and puffing, piled in with them, shielding her head with her arms.

The explosion was instant, deafening. They could feel it in the ground, in their guts. Bits of glass, wood, and masonry pinged and pummeled the alley walls. There were screams and shouts from up and down the street as debris rained down and after that, bedlam.

* * *

Scalarag ducked through the door to my small compartment with the evening meal on a tin plate. Though I'd been assigned to help prepare it, I was condemned to eat it in my quarters, my ankles in irons. The big man handed me the plate. I sat on my cot while he took the only chair. It seemed as if he might stay a while.

"Bless me father, for I have sinned."

What? This brute, now penitent? Our altercation must have made a deeper impression than I thought. Even so, having disgraced myself once through violence, I wasn't about to lie as well. "I'm sorry," I said. "I *was* a priest, but that was a long time ago."

"But you can still do the confession thing, can't you?"

He wasn't kidding. I told him, "Confession is always good for the soul, my son. I'm sure we can work something out."

He clasped his hands as if praying and looked mostly at the wall. "It has been . . . oh, ten, fifteen years since my last confession." Then he started confessing. It burst out of him. "My name isn't Scalarag, it's Tommy Bryce. I'm from Dubuque, Iowa, and I was a heavy equipment operator until I got in a fight and got fired and someone told me I ought to try out for the pirate show and so I ended up here. It started out being fun, all the pretending, the tourist show, the pirate ship. But you know, there's something about being a pirate. I mean, you start believing it, and then . . . there's just this wicked thing that happens."

"Like, for instance, an innocent tourist being locked in a cabin for reasons he doesn't know?"

Tommy nodded fervently. "Yeah, and ripping off the rich tourists. It's gotten out of hand, and now there could even be a murder."

There is *a God*, I thought — in jest, of course. "Ben?"

"Ben Cardiff. Seemed like a nice guy. He and the Captain were like *that*, but they still didn't trust each other. Cap could run the old satellite system, but then Ben did an upgrade to all the wireless internet stuff so he was the only one who knew how to run everything, all the Readers and Writers — but I guess I shouldn't say too much about that."

Oh, please do. "As you wish."

"But Ben had money problems and probably ended up being a traitor, trying to sell us out. He lit out Sunday night after our show, took all his stuff with him, and then . . . hey, if he made a deal with somebody it went south. They say Ben drowned, but the Cap saw Ben in the doc's freezer and somebody beat him to a pulp and tore the Reader out of his ear." He wagged his head. "It was bound to happen, that's what I'm saying. On this ship, the spoils go to the crafty and every man makes up his own rules. And it's a tough bunch. Rock used to be a drug dealer. Norwig got busted for armed robbery."

"So how does the Captain keep them all loyal?"

"As long as the takings are sweet they play along, but they're all looking for a better offer. Ben was, that's what we think." He leaned toward me. "Not that you and the Cap are friends, but I wouldn't stand too close to him. You never know what might be coming his way."

"Good advice, my son," I said, laying my hand upon his head.

He waited, then finally asked, "You gonna give me some penance or something?"

"Just tell God you're sorry. And do what's right."

LACEY AND DELILAH

Tank looked up and down the street. Folks were shaken, coated with dust, helping each other to their feet. A few were bleeding, but not seriously. No fatalities.

Lacey tugged his arm. "You've got to get out of here!"

"But people are hurt!"

"They'll live. You won't, not if you stay here!"

"But –"

"Get out of here!"

She tugged and urged Brenda, Tank, and Daniel until they ran headlong down the alley and didn't stop running until they'd regrouped in the living room of a comfortable bungalow a few blocks inland. Lacey drew the shades, then cracked one aside to double-check the street.

"What . . . what just happened?" Brenda asked, settling into a soft chair, holding Daniel close.

"Somebody tried to kill you by planting a bomb in my mom's restaurant," said Lacey, finally sitting in another chair. "In the kitchen, to be exact. It was set to go off at 6:01, and it did."

Tank figured the sofa would be okay and sat, speechless.

Brenda shuddered. "But . . . how did you . . . ?"

"You ought to know," said Lacey.

The back door opened.

"We're in here, mom," said Lacey.

In came the lady from the restaurant, the one who burst into the kitchen and told everyone to get out. She was bedraggled and dusty, and carrying a shopping bag.

"You okay?" asked Lacey.

"I'm all right," the lady answered, brushing a disturbed lock of hair from her face. "Everyone's okay. The insurance rep will be by tomorrow."

"So what caused it?"

The lady gave her head a cynical tilt. "They say it was a gas explosion."

"Oh, I'm *sure*!"

"Purely accidental, just a leaky gas line and then a spark somewhere set it off. In a kitchen with flames and cooking going on everywhere, a *spark* set it off?" She sat on the other end of the sofa and looked Brenda, Tank, and Daniel up and down. "So just who are you people, anyway?"

"Mom, this is Brenda, Daniel, and Tank. Brenda, Daniel, and Tank, this is my mom, Delilah."

"Pleased to meet you," said Tank.

Delilah still stared, even glared, at them. "So what was that movie line? 'Of all the restaurants in all the towns in all the world, you had to come into mine'?"

"Mom . . . "

"And into your store," she said to her daughter. "So first it was your boss, and now it's my restaurant. Why'd you send them to *my* place?"

Lacey was mortified. "I didn't think —"

"No, you didn't." Delilah reached into her shopping bag and pulled out a half-melted wall clock, it's glass face shattered. The hands indicated 6:01. "So how'd you know there was a bomb set to go off at exactly 6:01?"

Lacey pulled a scrap of paper from her shirt pocket — the paper on which Brenda had scribbled her and Tank's cell numbers. She turned it over to show Brenda's sketch on the reverse side: the very same half-melted wall clock with the glass shattered and the hands indicating 6:01.

Even Brenda was amazed. "I was just playing around with a Salvador Dali kind of thing."

"I grew up looking at that wall clock in the kitchen," said Lacey. "And when I saw this I thought of what happened to Mr. Moore after you and your friends came into the store, and I called Mom. I was going to call you next, but time got really tight."

"So that waitress who said we had a call?" Tank

asked.

"Never seen her before," said Delilah. "I was about to ask her what she was doing in my restaurant —and in my kitchen— but she ducked out, then Lacey called, then I put it together, and anyway . . . you saved my life and the lives of my staff— after putting us all in danger by walking into the restaurant in the first place."

"Mom . . . "

"So one more time, just who are you people? And who is it that wants to kill you and the rest of us over a stupid earring?"

Lacey explained to Brenda and Tank, "I didn't sell your friend the earring, but I saw Mr. Moore sell it to her, and then, Monday morning, after the pirate guy was killed, two men came into the store asking Mr. Moore about it: if he'd picked it up off the beach and if he still had it —"

Delilah broke in, "Neville Moore used to go out with a metal detector and find things on the beach in front of the resorts: jewelry, money, anything valuable. Then he'd take it back to his shop and turn right around and sell it. All the merchants knew about it, so those two men could have found out real easy."

"Anyway," Lacey continued, "that's where the earring came from. Mr. Moore found it on the beach under a tree and brought it back to the shop and ended up selling it to your friend Andi."

"What did the men look like?" Brenda asked.

"One was an older man, blond hair, dressed casual like a tourist. The other guy . . . " She cringed. "Big Asian guy, like a villain from a James Bond movie. They asked Mr. Moore to show them where he found it, so he went with them to show them, and the next thing we knew, Mr. Moore had drowned . . . just like the pirate guy."

"Ben Cardiff," said Tank.

Delilah nodded. "Which means you're in deep you-know-what."

Lacey explained, "Whoever those two men were, Mr. Moore told them about your friend Andi and where she and the rest of you were going. They know about you, they've probably been following you."

"You were lucky this time," said Delilah, "And I get a whole new kitchen if the insurance company pays up."

"But you don't know who they are?" asked Brenda.

Lacey exchanged a look with her mother and said, "Ever heard of The Gate?"

Delilah cautioned, "Shhh!"

Brenda and Tank could not conceal their shock. "We've, we've heard the term, yes," said Brenda, quite the understatement.

"Its the whisper around town," Delilah said guardedly. "With all the offshore banking that goes on here, a lot of money goes through this place, and a lot of dirty money too, and a lot of shadowy people. But we don't talk about it, do we, Lacey? We mind our own business and make our livings and stay out of the way."

"Well, we tried to," she admitted.

"Until you people stumbled in and stirred everything up. Guess it had to happen, though. Nobody here's got the guts to stand up to the . . . " She whispered it. "The Gate." Then she added at a cautious volume, "Whoever they are. Everybody's either bought or scared."

"But that's why maybe we should tell you—" Lacey hesitated.

"Say it, daughter." She nodded toward Brenda, Tank, and Daniel. "You never know, they might be here for a reason. Maybe they're the only ones who can break this thing open. Maybe *God* sent them."

"Wow," said Tank. "Cool!" Then Brenda gave him a corrective stare. "Sort of."

Lacey leaned forward. "A strange little man came into the shop with his wife about a month ago. He looked at jewelry, he looked at watches, he looked at scarves, he just looked at everything, and he liked some of it, he didn't like some of it, he talked about the colors and the styles of things. But the funny thing was, he was blind."

"He did the same thing at the Conch," said Delilah. "He saw the menu, looked at the choices, could read right off it without looking at it."

"Turns out it was his *wife*. She was doing all the looking and reading, and somehow he could see everything she was seeing. She'd look at a scarf and he'd comment on the size and the color. She'd look at a watch and he'd talk about the features he liked as if he could see it. It was like he was seeing through her eyes."

"So . . . how did they do it?" Tank asked.

"Don't know, but here's the connection: they were both wearing a big gold earring."

Brenda was fully alert now, spine straight. "Please say you have this guy's name, his number . . . "

"He bought a watch and a scarf . . . "

"And a lobster and steak," Delilah added.

"And we saved the receipts."

ZEDEKIAH SNOW

Wednesday morning, decked out in seaman's blouse and with a pirate scarf upon my head, I joined the crew, lending a hand and no small amount of muscle to hauling on the sheets and trimming the sails as the helmsman brought us about. While I had no intention of stooping to their level of savagery, it seemed my nearly breaking Scalarag's jaw had at least broken the ice and the crew were beginning to accept me, talking freely in my presence. The talk was, we were heading back for St. Clemens to do a Thursday show. What Thatch intended to do with Andi and me once we got there —or before we got there — was the foremost question of my day.

While I blended and sweated with the crew, Andi and Captain Thatch stood on the quarterdeck still digging for treasure in her memory.

"It was a money deal," she recalled, wide-eyed at the dawn of the recollection. "I . . . I mean, *Ben* . . . met with some people."

"Who?"

"Two guys, and they offered him a . . . Wow! A million up front, another million after delivery, all transferred into a secret bank account."

"HA! I can see it plain, the traitor!"

"Ben was trying to get out. They told him something like, It's all going to go down and you're going to go down with it unless you get out now. Get out, take the money, and disappear."

"Get out? Of what?"

Andi cringed as she shared it. "Whatever you pirates are doing."

"Two men? Who were they? Who were they working for?"

She shook her head. "I don't know."

The Captain put a finger in her face. "Faces. Would you know their faces if you saw them?"

She closed her eyes. "I might. I remember an older guy, and some big tough guy like a hit man. I think he was Asian . . . "

"Names?"

She shook her head. "Maybe they never told me . . . or Ben. But there was something else . . . " She winced, trying to remember.

"What, lass?"

"Something to do with a banana peel."

* * *

The receipts bore the name and signature of a certain Filbert Figg. A few discreet conversations among the St. Clemens merchants led Brenda and Tank to a shop owner who'd shipped some wind chimes to the same Mr. Figg. The shipping address was in Key West, Florida, the closely packed, miles-of-merchants tourist town that was once the haunt of Papa Hemingway. They caught a flight that morning and, after a cab ride through the busy streets and desultory throngs, found themselves at one of a row of houses crammed shoulder to shoulder along the waterfront. The particular model of wind chimes hanging near the front door confirmed they'd found the right place.

Brenda and Tank suspected the name Filbert Figg was an alias, and they were right. The name they'd cross-referenced to this address was actually Zedekiah Snow, and it was his wife Audrey who answered the door. She listened patiently to their story; when they described Andi's mysterious golden earring, she swung the door wide open. "Please come in. He'll want to hear this."

Zedekiah Snow was a small-framed, white haired man in a baseball cap, his eyes crazily disoriented, his visage scarred from an old injury. He appeared to be in the middle of a strange Eastern exercise in the center of the living room, leaning this way, then that, hands holding an invisible bar of some kind, shifting his weight as if negotiating fierce rapids.

"Zed . . . " said Audrey.

"Not now!"

"You have visitors."

"Tell them to go away!"

Audrey looked out the front windows. Brenda, Tank, and Daniel followed her gaze and spotted a sailboarder tacking across the wind and jumping the waves. Then they noticed how the sailboarder and Zedekiah Snow were making the very same moves at the very same time.

"Their friend just purchased one of Ben Cardiff's earrings," said Audrey. "And now she's been kidnapped."

As one, the old man and the sailboarder lost their balance and fell, the sailboarder into the waves, the old man onto the floor. As the sailboarder paddled about in the waves, the old man paddled on the floor, going nowhere. "How can that—? Oh, hold on!" He groped, then grabbed the bill of his hat, yanking it from his head and tossing it aside.

Now moving on his own, the sailboarder gathered up his board and started paddling for shore. Zedekiah Snow quit swimming and felt his way to a chair. He sat down and reached for a pair of dark glasses on the side table.

As he put them on, Audrey donned a pair of glasses from the kitchen counter and turned her gaze upon Brenda, Tank, and Daniel.

"Oh . . . " said Zedekiah, as if he were now seeing something through the glasses. "Looks like a family!"

Audrey introduced them as just friends.

"You're not from the government, are you?"

"No sir," said Tank. "We're just—"

"I won't talk to the government. And I thought I was hiding. How'd you find me?"

"Well . . . " Tank began.

"Never mind. Kidnapped? By whom?"

Tank and Brenda looked at each other. Daniel

answered, "Pirates!"

Audrey looked down at Daniel. Zedekiah reacted. "Cute kid. Pirates? Yes, that would be Ben, all right. Large gold earring, was it?"

Brenda and Tank brightened. "Yeah," said Brenda. "How'd she get it?"

"She bought it from a store on St. Clemens. The owner of the store was a scavenger and got it off the beach somewhere."

"Ha!" Snow must have been rolling his eyes behind those dark glasses. "So Ben's not as clever as he thinks."

"Sir, I'm sorry to tell you," said Tank, "Ben is dead. He was murdered."

Snow deflated a little, his hands plopping on the chair. "So now there's more to it. What about your friend? Did she wear the earring?"

"Oh yeah," said Brenda.

"Did she start behaving strangely?"

"She started acting like a pirate," said Tank.

"There *is* more to it. Better sit down and tell me the whole story."

They sat and spoke and Zedekiah Snow listened. When they'd recounted it all, including the kidnapping, the murders of Ben Cardiff and Neville Moore, and the bomb planted in the Conch restaurant, he took a moment to digest it, dry-washed his face, and said finally, "Well, your turn to hear my story, I suppose."

Audrey sat in another chair right next to him, looking at Brenda, Tank, and Daniel, as Zedekiah began. "You've gathered now, I can see you. Tank, the towering muscle man; Brenda, graceful carving in ebony; Daniel, the cherub with a special wisdom. It's coming into my brain through a Writer, a chip embedded in these glasses here." He tapped the dark glasses he wore. "And it's being sent from another chip, a Reader, in Audrey's glasses. She sees you, the image becomes brainwaves in her head; her glasses convert the brainwaves into a transmittable signal and send that signal through our translator system to my glasses. My glasses convert the signal back into brainwaves in my head, and my brain translates them back into the image she sees. Very simple concept."

The beachside door opened, and the sailboarder came in.

"Ah! My son Jeremiah! No doubt you noticed our little experiment. We were sailboarding together. Jeremiah, how'd it go?"

The young man was wet and tired, but pleased. "Weird. Like I was you."

"And you were me!" Zedekiah laughed. To Brenda, Tank and Daniel, "The very first bi-directional mind feed! He sends me his sensory impressions through a Reader in his headband, I pick them up through a Writer in that billed cap over there and send back my rusty old skills in riding a sailboard. With bi-directional feed, we share the experience!"

"The problem was deciding just who was driving," said Jeremiah.

"That can be worked out with practice and mutual agreement. But you see how wonderful this could be? The blind can see through the eyes of their loved ones; the deaf can hear, the paralyzed can walk and old blind cranks like me can even ride a sailboard through the mind and senses of someone else!"

"It's incredible!" said Brenda.

Zedekiah Snow sank back in his chair. "Mm, and

it's also dangerous, as you have discovered. Your friend Andi has experienced far more than she wanted . . . just as I feared would happen some day. Ben Cardiff and I were associates. Together we perfected the Read/Write system. It was Ben's idea to plant the Reader and Writer chips in head garments. It held great promise for the blind, the deaf, anyone else who might be denied a fuller life experience. But Ben was a moral weakling, and he came across a scoundrel willing to exploit that weakness: Horatio Thatch?"

Tank and Brenda didn't recognize the name . . . at first.

"*Captain* Horatio Thatch?"

Their eyes widened. "The captain from the pirate show!"

"A pirate indeed," said Snow. "For the tourists and . . . a pirate of a very different kind when it comes to pirating the minds of rich tourists to gain access to their bank accounts and portfolios. Thatch wooed Ben away from me with promises of using our invention to get rich, and, I suppose, that's what's happened. Place a pirate hat or an earring or a scarf on a tourist to take a pirate picture, and while they're smiling and making a memory, all their bank information is downloaded directly from their brain. That's why Audrey and I were on St. Clemens a month ago — secretly, we thought. We were checking out what use Ben and Thatch were making of our Read/Write system. Now . . . oh dear, what to do? No doubt you've gone to the authorities?" Amazingly, he could see the look on their faces. "Ha! That's what I thought. The Gate's already been there. Ohhhh, yes, I know about The Gate. They came to me first, wanting the system. Sell *them* the system? They'd make worse use of it than the government, prying, spying, pirating! I became Filbert Figg and vanished. But Ben was still available, I see. He cut a deal, I suppose, and the deal went south somehow—" Suddenly he appeared stricken by a revelation. "Ahhhh yes! Would you like to hear an excellent guess?"

Brenda and Tank nodded knowing he could see them.

"Ben struck a deal to sell The Gate the technology. To show what it could do, he left a Writer earring at a drop point on the beach for The Gate to pick up. Then, wearing the Reader earring himself, he intended to transfer his memory, all the vital information, to The Gate through the system, his Reader to the Writer they supposedly had. Except . . . "

Tank spoke the conclusion, "Except Neville Moore the shopkeeper found it first, and Andi got the earring instead!"

"And so The Gate was out their money and thought Ben had swindled them, so Ben came to an ignominious end, and now . . . " Zedekiah laughed, either at the trickery of the events or at his own cleverness. "And now, it is not The Gate who has all of Ben's knowledge and the technology, and it's not Thatch and his pirates either; it is Andi who has it all in her head!" Then he stopped laughing. "Oh dear. That doesn't bode well for her, does it?"

THE WILD MAN

That evening, I was back in leg irons in my compartment, awaiting dinner. The irons could have been a stage prop at one time, but they were functional now, rendering me helpless. I suspected, I hoped, that their ultimate function was to encourage Andi's cooperation and nothing beyond that.

But by now I just couldn't be sure.

* * *

"We've been good to your friend the prof," the Captain told Andi. "Each day, each hour he's still breathing, he'll have you to thank for it. Remember that."

Andi was seated before the computer screen again, looking through screens, menus, drop-downs, with the Captain and Sparks looking over her shoulder. "It all looks familiar."

His hand was on her shoulder. "We need the numbers, the pass codes to access the bank accounts."

"Don't you have them written down somewhere?"

"Ben did, and now he's gone and the records with him."

"So . . . " Andi kept looking. "Looks like you can't always have it your way after all."

His grip on her shoulder tightened. It hurt. "Don't let that thought cross your mind. I'll have what I want."

Well, everyone has their tipping point. Andi was reaching hers. Even while grimacing with the pain she told him, "As if brute force is going to make you right in the grand scheme of things?" She twisted in her chair to look him in the eye, batting away his grip. "You may be captain of this ship, but it's a mighty big ocean. You may scoff at God and Truth, but this system runs on Truth, on rules of physics and mathematics that must be obeyed whether you like it or not, and if I'm going to solve this problem it's going to be according to those rules, not yours. Now *back off!*"

As if grudgingly conceding her point, he straightened, giving her space, and crossed his arms, removing physical threat. "Well then. Where do we stand according to these . . . *rules?*"

As if the momentary distraction had freed up her mind, she thought of using another path to the files. She scrolled, she clicked. "Oh, oh, ohhh, looky here!"

"Ah!"

"Recognize them?"

"Yes!" He chuckled and this time patted her shoulder.

Sparks patted her other shoulder. "These are the bank accounts, with their codes!"

She began to scroll down the screen. "Yes! This is the code for Switzerland . . . and this is the code for France . . . for England . . . Japan . . . Germany . . . and this link takes you to the server in New York. Wow!"

"Keep going, lass," said the captain. Then he added chillingly, "Professor McKinney is counting on you."

She rolled her eyes but he didn't see it.

There was a commotion below, enough to make the beams quiver: Blows, boots, the clatter of a plate, the creak of an old door. There was that scream again! Footsteps thundered up the passage just outside.

The Captain bolted to the door. "Scalarag! What's-_"

A body collided with the Captain and he reeled into the passageway. For a terrifying instant, a ragged wraith leaned in the doorway, eyes white and crazy, hair an explosion, squeaking out a laugh and babbling gibberish as the air carried the stench of feces and urine. Andi shied back into a corner. Sparks grabbed up a chair to shield himself.

With a maniacal cry, the creature bolted, leaped over the fallen Captain and ran up the passage, and it was only now that Andi realized who it was — Jean-Pierre DuBois, the flamboyant French buccaneer! He'd not been seen since the Captain handed him Andi's gold earring and he took it below decks. Moments after that came the first scream, undoubtedly from this same wretch who was clearly out of his mind.

"Spikenose!" the Captain bellowed.

The little cook, nose bleeding, bounded up the passageway. "He jumped me! I was bringing him his dinner and he jumped me!"

"All hands," yelled the Captain. "Lay hold of that madman!"

"Captain!"

Thatch looked at Spikenose impatiently.

"He has my pistol!"

Both men thundered up the passageway and Sparks followed as the whole ship came alive with shouts, stomps, running.

Andi, overwhelmed with curiosity, hurried topside in time to see Norwig the Bean and Sparks sprawled on the deck, second best in a tangle with DuBois the maniac who now scrambled about the deck and up to the forecastle, chased by Rock and Scalarag. DuBois was swinging from the shrouds, hurling things, screaming, laughing. Finally, with Rock and Norwig guarding one set of steps and Scalarag and Sparks the other, he was trapped on the forecastle. The Captain stepped forward and tried to talk sense, but DuBois drew Spikenose' pistol from his belt and took aim. The Captain ducked aside just as the weapon went off with a loud report and a puff of blue smoke. A lead ball blasted a splinter out of the main mast, ricocheted off the deck and broke out a window of the Captain's quarters.

At that, Captain Thatch drew his own pistol even as DuBois drew a sizable knife. Stepping up on the rail, DuBois leaped at the Captain.

The Captain fired. DuBois took a lead ball through the neck and tumbled onto the deck squirting blood.

Andi looked away.

When she looked again, the Captain stood over DuBois, cursing. The men came running. Scalarag knelt by the Frenchman trying to stop the bleeding, but the damage was done, exceedingly. Rock looked at DuBois, at the Captain. "Those . . . those were live rounds!"

The Captain slowly replaced his pistol. "Spare me the act, Rock. You're not surprised." He looked around the horrified circle, eyeing their pistols. "Nor any of the rest of you, I'll wager!"

Scalarag stood, blood all over him. DuBois was dead.

"He was my friend," said the Captain. "It was Ben did this to him, but we've made it square."

"What . . . " Norwig was trembling. "What are we gonna do?"

The Captain started for his quarters. "Think it through, mates. I have. We hold course for St. Clemens. There's big money to be made."

"But . . . " said Rock, "what about—?"

"Tie him to some weights and throw him over the side."

TAKING THE RIQUEZA

At Zedekiah and Audrey's insistence, Brenda, Tank, and Daniel had dinner and spent the night. Brenda crashed on the couch, Tank on the floor, Daniel on the floor next to Tank and close to Brenda. Sleep, at least for Tank, was a little difficult with the frequent vibrations coming through the floor: Zedekiah, bothered and thinking, pacing back and forth from his bedroom to his computer room and back again.

In the morning, over bagels and fresh-brewed coffee, he shared his musings. "A kidnapping from a lonely beach and a boat rowed out to sea? Not The Gate's style, but definitely the style of Thatch and his pirates. Also, the murders tell me The Gate doesn't yet have the technology, while we know Thatch and his pirates do. Therefore . . . "

With Audrey as his eyes, he led them into his computer room, a chaotic jumble of keyboards, screens, wires, control panels, and papers, all labeled for Audrey's sake with post-it notes. "If we assume the Read/Write technology interfaces wirelessly with either a satellite or the internet, I might be able to hack into the system aboard that ship. If we can pick up a signal from any Reader, the GPS inside the Reader will tell us where the ship is, and if . . . " He hesitated.

"If . . . what?" Brenda asked.

Zedekiah opened a drawer and produced a gold earring exactly like the one Andi had bought and worn. "Yes, Ben and I made several of these, both Readers and Writers. This one is a Writer, and if one of us can wear it, we could possibly connect with a Reader aboard the *Predator* and . . . uh . . . receive mental impressions of the surroundings, maybe even overhear conversations, see who and what we're dealing with."

"Yeah!" said Tank. "That's it! Can we do that?"

"Well, in a perfect world, yes. But someone on the *Predator* would have to be wearing the Reader in order for us to receive their mental images. We'd be fishing a bit."

Brenda could hear the uneasiness in his voice. "Okay, what else?"

"I have no control over the system on the ship. If Ben or anyone else has scrambled or encrypted the system to prevent invasion, this Writer could, uh, scramble the brain of the wearer." He nervously cleared his throat. "The damage would be irreparable."

* * *

I awoke that morning to a new sensation: the rumble of engines! So much for the seventeenth century.

I had little time to wonder about it before Scalarag ducked through the compartment door. "Up and about, Professor! We've a show to do today! Deck yourself out as befits a seaman." He produced the key to the leg irons and set me free. "Cap wants all men on deck. We've set course to overtake the *Riqueza*."

Ah yes, the *Riqueza*, the colorful and completely fake Spanish galleon I and the team had climbed aboard less than a week ago. Within hours it would be loaded with laughing, gawking tourists with cameras and piña coladas, all ready to be boarded and raided by make-believe pirates. Oh, if those hapless flower shirts only knew!

Donning my seaman's blouse and pirate's scarf, I followed Scalarag topside, emerging on the deck to find the sails unfurling, the crew hauling and trimming to wring out the utmost knot.

"You!" hollered Rock. "On the mizzen!"

"The third mast," Scalarag advised me.

I hurried to join the crew, taking hold of the sheets and letting them out to open the sails fully to the wind. The *Predator* heeled to port, the waves dashing and foaming against her sides. We were motoring *and* sailing, in a hurry.

Thatch stood by the rail at the bow, sighting ahead with a spyglass. "There she lies!"

I could see the three-masted *Riqueza* on the horizon, only half her sails unfurled, poking along to be taken by the likes of us.

"Look alive, men! Cast loose the guns!"

There were six cannons on the main deck, lashed, tied, and chocked. The gunners let them loose.

Scalarag led me to a locker beneath the quarterdeck where we found folding chairs. We formed a chain with some of the crew and set them up on the quarterdeck, twenty in all. These would be the choice seats for the tourists with red wrist bands.

"Load your guns!"

With practice and polish, the gunners put the powder cartridges and wadding down each bore and rammed them home. No cannon balls; this was show biz, just smoke and noise.

We were closing on the galleon, and dead ahead of us both was Pirate Island, a green bump in the ocean where a Disneyesque Port Royal awaited with costumed staff, souvenir stores, and pirate dinner show.

"Fire!"

From the deck of the *Riqueza* the cannon fire had been exciting and theatrical. From where I stood on the *Predator*, it was a fusillade of thunders that shook the boat and made jello of my insides.

"Reload!"

I could see the *Riqueza* was laden with brightly clad, sun-blocked tourists, no doubt wealthy, a veritable treasure trove — the admission price for this fantasy made sure of that.

The cannons would be firing again. This time I would unabashedly cover my ears.

*   *   *

Zedekiah tapped the keys while Audrey watched the computer monitor. "We'll send out an inquiry and see if we get a reply from any Readers aboard the *Predator*. I'd like to go around the ship's system so nobody notices, but . . . well, here goes anyway."

"I think there was a show scheduled for today," said Audrey.

"Oo-hoo, then we might see quite a spectacle . . . or somebody will."

Audrey looked at Tank; he just wondered why. She looked at Brenda; Brenda cringed a bit.

Zedekiah muttered to himself, kept tapping the keys, moving the mouse around. "Elusive little devils . . ."

* * *

Andi sat at the console, letting one memory lead to another as she strived to get the system working.

Sparks sat in a chair beside her, more a snoop and a nuisance than a help. "Come on, we have to get the Readers linked up before we dock." He pointed at a small blinking box near the top corner of the screen. "Is that an inquiry?"

The moment Andi saw it, she knew what it was. "Shouldn't be. Is there a Writer energized somewhere?"

Sparks checked the cabinet where the Writers — some earrings, a hat, a very modern headset — were kept. Just then the whole ship quaked as the boom of the cannons rang through the timbers. Sparks braced himself. He was looking away.

With a quick sequence of clicks, Andi consigned the blinking box to another screen which she minimized out of sight. "No, forget it, looks like we're clear. Must have been something else."

"What?"

"When I remember, I'll tell you."

* * *

It was the finest entertainment, really: Muscular

men in pirate garb, swords flashing, pistols popping, swinging on ropes like acrobats, swarming aboard the *Riqueza* and playfully taking captive the extra-paying tourists with a red wrist band. I joined in the fun, blending, as it were, helping the hapless souls across the gangplank and aboard the *Predator*. With roguish decorum, I showed a jolly couple to their chairs.

"Oh," said the lady, "I'll bet you have fun being a pirate!"

"M'lady," I said as I took their drink orders, "you have no idea!"

* * *

Zedekiah Snow shook his head as Audrey, his eyes, scanned the computer screen. "No, no, we aren't getting through. This has to be the ship's system, it's framed just the way Ben would have done it, but it won't let us past the initial inquiry. It can hear us knocking at the door, but it's waiting for the password to let us in."

"Wait a minute," said Tank, pulling a notepad from his pocket. "What about what Andi said that first time, the aardvark thing?" He flipped through the pages until he found it. "Uh, Aardvark, Basil, Crustacean, 233 —"

"Hold on, hold on!" said Snow, tapping away at the keys. "Now, is that just A, B, C, or the whole words?"

"I don't know."

"We'll try the whole words." He tapped them in. "Now, you have numbers?"

"233 997 417709."

Snow tapped them in. "Mmm. Ben always liked big entry codes. Here goes." He tapped **Enter**.

They waited.

THE MIND PIRATES

AN INQUIRY

Thatch was in full character, strutting about the deck, sword waving above his head, wild-eyed and savage. "You'll be taking your seats and causing us no grief, or we'll sever the tendons behind your knees, roll you up in squid guts and throw you to the sharks!"

Our captives laughed at that. Context was everything.

I brought up the last couple, definitely self-made high rollers judging from the man's watch.

Rock took his turn letting the chosen twenty know where the restrooms and life jackets were, and from that point, as both ships eased into the lagoon and toward the wharf at Pirate Island, there were songs, demonstrations, even a member of the crew who could juggle knives with his ankles behind his neck. I could never do that.

* * *

Andi knew, thanks to Ben's memory, that another system was trying to link up with the system on the ship. She also knew such a fact could be an advantage if Sparks didn't know about it. "Okay, this must be the codes and frequencies for the Readers. Where are they?"

"In the Captain's quarters," said Sparks. "They go ashore when we dock."

"Well, I need the identifier for each one so I can keep track of what I'm monitoring."

"Should be on your screen."

"I can't find it."

"We're pulling up to the wharf!"

She faced him and shrugged with palms up, at a loss.

That got him to move. "I'll get the info off the units. Hold on." He hurried out of the room, heading topside.

She had her chance, a window of mere minutes. Hurriedly, she brought up the blinking box. One click and it became a menu, and within that menu was an inquiry. Somewhere, someone was requesting access to the Readers — and with that request was the access code, the words Aardvark, Basil, Crustacean, and the numerical sequence.

Oh! It was like being able to breathe again, to live just one more moment. This was the outside world calling, the only people who would know this access code: Tank, Brenda, Daniel!

Come on, come on, she pleaded with Ben's memory, how do I accept?

All she had to do was ask; the memory came to her. She clicked here, entered a command there, assigned a path, and clicked EXECUTE.

* * *

"We're in!" said Zedekiah Snow with a clap of his hands.

Tank let out a whoop.

Brenda asked, "What does that mean?"

"It means," said Zedekiah, "that now we can use a Writer at this end to receive brainwaves from a Reader at their end, to tap into what's going on."

"Great!" said Tank.

Brenda was rather quiet.

Zedekiah got a little quiet himself. "And the fact that user input was necessary to complete the access tells me that someone running the system let us in."

"Andi!" said Daniel.

* * *

Andi could see the code going through, the system responding —

"Are we ready?" came the Captain's voice behind her.

It made her jump. She rose from the chair, fumbled for the mouse, blocked the screen with her body. "Uh . . . uh, yeah, I think so. Uh, Sparks has gone up to get the identifiers from the Readers."

How long had he been standing there? Did he see the inquiry, the access code? Were they still on the screen?

Well of course they were! She was dead. Fried.

What was he holding? Some green, feathery outfit. "Try this on for size."

"Uh, right, right. Just let me make sure . . . " Her hand trembled as she moved and clicked the mouse. The menu closed, but the system was acknowledging the inquiry, opening up all the Readers — both on the ship and . . . wherever else. Sparks was sure to notice.

Speak of the devil. Sparks came back in with a list in his hand. "Okay, here are the identifiers —" He spotted the screen and pushed her aside. "Well, looks like you found them."

"Uh, yeah. Up and running as far as I can tell."

He sat in the chair. "Okay, Readers are online, ready to go ashore."

"Aye, and in good time," said the Captain. "Norwig will set them up. Got my Writer?" Sparks reached for a gold earring hanging on a hook and handed it to the Captain. "Grand enough. Tell me when I can listen in."

"Will do."

The Captain addressed Andi, "And as for you . . . " He handed her the green, feathery thing. "You m'lady, will accompany me."

"What's this?" had just escaped her lips when she saw the cartoonish parrot head and realized it was a costume.

"Being the parrot always falls to Spikenose, but not today," said the Captain. "Today, it falls to you. I'll not be leaving you aboard the ship unwatched, nor can I let your face be seen, so today you're the parrot."

"Happy squawking, shipmate," said Sparks, his glee all too evident as he turned to the console. "I'll take it from here."

* * *

"Yes, yes, of course," said Zedekiah, still clicking

and tapping for information. "The *Predator*'s GPS locator places the ship at Pirate Island. No surprise there. You were right, Audrey, they must have a show today."

"But that just proves you're into the *Predator*'s system!" said Tank.

"With the help of someone who recognized the access code, and that it could only come from you. Now if we can just pick up a Reader. Maybe your friend Andi will see to that . . . "

Daniel always meant well, and I imagine he could discern Brenda's misgivings about the magical earring. While all the others were focused on what was happening on Pirate Island, he gently took the earring from the table and looked it over.

"I think I'm finding some of the Readers . . . " Zedekiah said.

The screen went crazy!

"Oh!" said Audrey.

"Oh, no, no, no!" said Zedekiah.

Daniel didn't have pierced ears. He may have thought he would hear something by pressing the earring to his ear.

"Someone's scrambled the system!" said Zedekiah, and perhaps the one great fear that came with that made Audrey scan the room for the earring. "Daniel!" she cried.

"Daniel, stop!" Zedekiah screamed.

Brenda's hand grabbed Daniel's wrist when the earring was only inches from his head and plucked the earring from his hand. As if it were red hot, she tossed the earring to the floor. Daniel was terribly frightened, of course, on the verge of tears, but she pulled him close. "It's okay, baby, it's okay . . . "

Zedekiah settled, shaking, into his chair. He had to clear his throat before he could say, "Audrey, if you please, the screen."

She returned to her post beside him and looked at the screen.

Zedekiah slumped in his chair. "Where we once had a friend, we now have an enemy. Don't touch that earring."

PIRATE ISLAND

Pirate Island. It was pure fantasy, a seaport in miniature harking back to the Caribbean of the seventeenth century with its colonialism and rowdy decadence. As a tourist, I'd found it amusing. Now, save for my perilous situation, I could have been a part of it. Even as Scalarag and I helped secure the dock lines to moor the *Predator* safely against the wharf, I was enchanted by the village, the costumed populace, the seafaring music, the smell of the sea, and the majestic sailing ships. If I'd not been a captive I could have been living in another time, caught up in the euphoria of make-believe.

As were the tourists, I suppose, coming down the gangways and flooding the place, cell phones and cameras already clicking at the sights: the wenches peddling their goods, the jugglers, the fire eater, the traditional dancers, Captain Thatch in full regalia accompanied by his theme park parrot.

* * *

Andi did her best to be a parrot, waddling on her parrot feet and looking out through the cartoonish, two-way eyes, but her mind was on the system, the inquiry, Sparks sitting there watching that screen.

The Captain drew the gold earring from his pocket as he strutted and Andi waddled up to the Pirate Island photo booth next to the wharf. Here the tourists could don the pirate hats, scarves, and earrings from the rack and get a souvenir photo with the Captain, the *Predator* filling the background. Norwig the Bean was running the booth; Harry the Scar was the photographer.

And right now, they were idle.

"Well?" asked the Captain.

"Ready when you are," said Norwig.

"Before the show, then. We'll —" Thatch winced and put his finger to his ear. "What? Say again?" He was wearing an earbud to keep in radio contact with Sparks. It appeared Sparks was talking to him. "Why? We're not taking any pictures yet. All the Readers are hanging on the rack in a dead calm." He glanced at the earring in his hand and told Norwig, "Sparks says to put on the earring, we're getting a signal."

Norwig and Harry looked again at the rack of scarves, hats, and earrings, all the Readers they had. "From what?" asked Norwig.

Thatch radioed back, "All the Readers are right here, doing nothing . . . well, you give me a Read and I'll put on the Writer!"

He shoved the earring back in his pocket. "Keeps

telling me to put on the earring. I hate that thing, and what's to monitor?"

"But have you noticed," said Harry, "how many scarves and hats there are already?"

The Captain looked about, and so did Andi, and Harry had a point. All along the wharf, across the dining plaza, and up the length of the cobblestone street, heads without a scarf or pirate hat of some kind were few and far between.

"So why should they wear one of ours?" asked Norwig.

"What about the mark?"

"Aye, we met him. Mr. Ling. Cold as ice and not to be tangled with."

The Captain gave that pill time to go down. "Ling, you say? And where might he be?"

"Scarfing some barbecue." Norwig jerked his thumb toward the dining plaza.

The Captain, with Andi in tow, hurried back onto the wharf. "Gentlemen!" Scalarag and I snapped to a ragged attention. "You'll return to the ship. Scalarag, we'll be about a new business now. Have the prof lend a hand, and keep him under your watchful eye." To me, "Sorry, prof. Still need to keep your pretty assistant in the right frame of mind, and . . . can't have you talking or passing notes to anyone, now can we?"

The parrot gave me a little wave and a lingering look as it walked beside the Captain toward the village. Well. Of course Thatch would want her under his control at all times. Andi was falling into the role, waving, squawking, posing for pictures beside her flamboyant master.

And what could I do as a prisoner? A hostage?

Insurance to keep Andi in line? As Scalarag escorted me up the gangplank my anger was getting the better of me. "So what now? Leg irons again? More humiliation while the silly game goes on?"

"No," Scalarag answered.

"And to think at one time you had a conscience!"

"I said *No*. No leg irons. Plan B."

I looked back at him. He nudged me onto the deck where we were unseen by those ashore. "The Cap has a nose for trouble and we might be in it. We have to load the cannons."

"What!?"

He led the way below, toward the front of the hold. "You told me to do the right thing. Well, this is the right thing." He stopped and faced me. "To my way of thinking, anyway."

He hurried onward, I followed. He came to a secure door, unlocked it, and flung it open. Inside were barrels upon barrels neatly stacked, each bearing the label National Munitions Inc.

I'd seen a few of these barrels topside during the mock cannon firing. "Gunpowder?"

He gazed at the huge cache with visible awe and nodded. "Let's each grab one."

"But . . . you're not going to . . . "

He hefted one into my arms. "If the Captain says so."

"But what puts *him* in the right?"

"The guns, I suppose."

* * *

We loaded the cannons on the landward side — they were aimed right at the plaza where most of the crowds had gathered.

Of course I wondered what the devil I was doing,

aiding and abetting a pack of scoundrels, or at least one scoundrel and his accomplice, but then again, Andi was out there in the company of the Captain, and if any plan to save the Captain would save *her* . . .

There had to something right about that.

Regardless, pragmatically speaking, whatever action we took had to be preset without delay if it were to succeed when the time came, so having no time to fret about moralities, I helped fill the powder bags and rammed them down the bores.

Ammunition? Blast Scalarag! He drew a blank and left that up to me.

* * *

Andi could smell barbecue even through her parrot head. The dining plaza was a town square with a clear view of the wharf and the ships tied there. Folks sat at tables while the serving wenches scurried about with trays of drinks and sandwiches.

At a lone table on the edge of the plaza, two men sat having lunch and a beer. Thatch made a bee line for that table. "Keep up," he told Andi, "and have a good look at these two." She kept up. He circled around the table to face the two men, she stayed beside him . . .

And walked right into her nightmare, right into *that night:* the wrinkly blond man with death in his eyes. The stone-faced Asian with the gleaming knife. Running for her life as Ben Cardiff ran for his, her body, his body, pummeled and thrown to a slow, drowning death.

There they sat, the blond man, the big Asian man, looking so casual, nibbling on sandwiches, sipping beer. Thatch engaged the blond man in conversation about booking tour groups for the pirate show, how well the season was going, where all these extra hats and scarves came from. She couldn't concentrate on the words, only on not shaking, not fainting, not screaming.

The blond man introduced Mr. Ling, a big investment banker from Hong Kong. Ling looked just as Norwig described him: cold as ice and ruthless. He looked at Andi only once and, seeing only a silly parrot, looked back at the Captain. The Captain was suggesting a group picture, perhaps with an official *Predator* Captain's hat. The killer smiled as if he knew something.

The blond man smiled too. Lots of tour groups lined up, he said, very good gate this weekend. He had a shirt with ST. CLEMENS TOURS embossed over the pocket, and above the embossing he wore a name badge: Bennett Piel.

Bennett Piel!

Her legs lost their strength. She stumbled backward a few waddled steps, reached and found a palm tree to steady herself.

Banana Peel!

MUTINY

A sound, something like a cry, escaped Andi's mouth before she could contain it. She disguised it with a parrot squawk. She flapped her arms a little. It drew a look and an impatient smile from Bennett Piel.

The Captain brought up future plans and recovered Piel's attention.

Come on, act like a parrot. With all she had within her she stayed in character, *awked* a little, and sidled away to give them space, to come up with a plan . . .

To get to a buffet table and a bowl of fruit.

She squawked a greeting to two dining couples — the women were the ugliest she'd seen in a while — and helped herself to a banana.

She waddled back, moving behind the two men and facing the Captain.

Thatch talked with the men about the *Predator*. A good ship, she was. Ready for haul out next month.

He had improvements in mind, budget allowing.

She held up the banana hoping he would see it.

He may have. Apparently he was getting another message from Sparks. He took the earring out of his pocket.

She grappled and fumbled with the banana. It was hard to get the peeling started with feathery parrot wing hands.

The Captain pulled his hair back to expose his ear and then began to open the loop on the earring.

She got the peeling started and frantically pulled the segments down.

He looked at her.

With the banana peeled halfway down, she pointed at it while pointing at Bennett Piel with the feathery finger of her other hand. *That's the guy!*

The Captain stayed in character, smiling, listening to the two men, looking from one to the other as the color drained from his face. He put the earring back in his pocket, and managing a weakened flourish, said, "Gentlemen, ado, and fair winds!"

He beckoned to Andi with a glance and started walking—back toward the ship. Andi was glad enough to follow.

They didn't get far.

"Thatch!" Piel shouted from behind them. With that came the clicking of a gun.

Click! Clack! Clicklick Clatter! Like dozens of traps springing, the tourists, male and female, sprang from their chairs and trained their guns on Thatch's crew. Others on the rim of the plaza formed a closed circle, brandishing weapons. The ugly women turned out to be men, their hairy arms holding pistols.

"You won't be walking off that easy," said Bennett

Piel.

Thatch and Andi turned slowly. Piel stood gloating. So did Mr. Ling.

The Captain didn't seem surprised. "So it's as I hear: 'We laugh at honor and are shocked to find traitors in our midst.'"

"Honor can't stand up to a lucrative arrangement," said Piel. "The smart ones know a better deal when it's offered."

"Smart and a murderin' scum! A big money man from Hong Kong, is he? 'Twas you and Ling pitched Ben Cardiff to the brine!"

"If it's any consolation, we didn't mean to kill him. But he did take us for a million!" He nodded toward Mr. Ling. "Nevertheless, my friend here has promised me a fat future to finish this business any way we can. Mr. Ling wants your ship, Thatch, and all that gadgetry you have onboard!"

The Captain studied Mr. Ling a moment. "The Gate, I presume? I've heard tell of you around St. Clemens, and oh, you can persuade, I'll lay to that." The Captain met the eyes of his men, then looked at Piel and Ling. "But will you leave a bloodied island for the law to find?" The Captain slowly drew his pistol. "That we'll try." He advised the costumed servers and staff, "I'd find cover inside."

He didn't have to tell them twice.

Thatch's crew drew their period weapons, clicking back the hammers all around, their muzzles mirroring the muzzles aimed at them.

* * *

From the deck of the *Predator*, Scalarag and I could see the frozen tableau of some fifty mock tourists brandishing weapons and Thatch's crew brandishing weapons right back.

"This is insane!" I said.

"This is money," said Scalarag. "Thatch guessed right. Someone made Piel a better offer."

The Gate, I thought. This was their sneaky style. "They . . . they can't just kill each other!"

"Neither has a winning hand, so who knows where it goes from here?"

Oh, Andi! She had such a gift for being caught in the middle. "Cheerios," I said.

"What?"

"Ammunition for the cannons. We have Cheerios."

* * *

Mr. Ling broke into a smile. "So now we parlay, eh? And what have you to bargain with, Thatch?" He spoke loudly so all could hear, "Men of the *Predator*! Whatever Thatch is paying, I'll make it double. All I want is that ship and what's aboard. Hand it over and walk away alive — and richer!"

There was a telling pause. Both sides still aimed their weapons, but Thatch's men were thinking about it.

"Mutiny . . . " a crewman muttered.

"Mutiny?" bellowed the Captain, striding before them. "And go home lesser men? Can honor be bought that easily?"

* * *

Rock leaped to the first large limb of a tree, waved his sword and hollered out, "Why stand you all tangled in the stays? Was it honor filled your purses? The *gold's* the thing, mateys, and gold buys the wiser! Take it now, live to tell it, and live happy! Mutiny!"

There was a cheer, but it was half-hearted.

* * *

A knife came from somewhere and pinned Rock's sleeve to the tree! That drew everyone's attention to none other than Norwig the Bean, standing near the Captain. He jerked his head at Piel and Ling. "And you'll believe the word of scum like these, when the first word is pistols up your nose? What do you know, mates, if it ain't the Captain and *his* word? I say we stick by the old man and let tomorrow come as always! Mutiny against the mutiny!"

Another cheer, but that was half-hearted too.

* * *

Oof! Spikenose, like a wiry little spider on a web, swung in on a rope and kicked Norwig aside, taking his place in the center. He had a pistol in one hand and a saber in the other and twirled them both to get attention, which he got. "Come on, guys, get a clue! Thatch has been using all of us to make himself rich and The Gate only wants to kill us and take what's ours! Can't you see this whole thing is falling apart? This whole pirate thing, it's over, and I'm sick of it anyway! Listen! I'm the purser with signatory rights on the bank account. Let's split the company assets and get out. Let Thatch and The Gate fight over the rest! Mutiny against the mutiny against the mutiny!"

That brought an intelligent murmur.

* * *

Harry the Scar stepped into the center and gave a shrill whistle. The murmuring stopped. "Just walk away with the money, is that it? That simple? Any of you want to lay me odds the feds aren't onto us by now? They've gotta be tracking these Gate guys and they've got to know where most of our money's come from. You don't think they're all over us too? Listen, we didn't invent the technology, right? We were just working the ship, doing the shows, right? But we know about the Captain and now we know about The Gate, so let's go to the feds, turn 'em in, and cut a deal." He had to count on his fingers as he said, "Mutiny against the mutiny against the mutiny against the mutiny!"

* * *

What was this, *parlay ad absurdum?* Andi looked around, wondering who was going to speak next when –

AWK! A huge hand from behind grabbed her by the scruff of her costume.

It was Sparks' voice! "All this blabbering and you don't know what's right under your nose!"

He held her, half hanging, by her costume, her parrot feet barely touching the ground. OUCH! He yanked the goofy parrot head off her and tossed it aside. Her unconstrained hair exploded from her head like a red firework.

Most everyone gave a little gasp or mutter at the sight of her, but Piel and Ling stood silent as lights came on behind their eyes. Piel even mouthed the words, "The redheaded girl!"

"Ah," said Sparks, "so you know what I'm holding!" He put a knife to her neck! "Here's the real prize: Everything Ben knew and you paid for, it's in her head — and that includes where your million dollars went. So here's my offer: Make me captain. Give me the crew and the *Predator*, and we'll come over to your side and hand you the girl." He dragged her around a little, making sure all the crew could see the prize and his knife to her throat. "Can't make up your minds? Take a good look at her! Follow me, I follow them, they get the girl, we keep the *Predator* and we all get richer."

Spikenose looked into space, counting, "A mutiny against the mutiny against the mutiny . . . "

"Shut up!"

* * *

There must have been something about a knife to her throat that Andi found disagreeable. With abandon and bravado she must have learned from Ben, she burst out, "By the powers, ya swab, you're as sharp as paint, you are! Be the captain? Is that why it was you scrambled the system and Jean-Pierre's brain? You were hoping the Cap would put on that earring as always, but Jean-Pierre wore it that day, and 'twas his bad fortune!"

He tightened his grip. "Hold your tongue or I'll cut it out."

"And toss it to Piel and Ling? Oh, they'll pay you well for that!"

Click! Oh, how she hated that sound!

Sparks spun around, dragging her around with him.

The Captain was pointing his pistol at Sparks, steady, steely-eyed. In his free hand he held the earring. "So that's why you hoped I'd put on the earring today. You were planning for me what fell to Jean-Pierre." He shouted to the men of the *Predator*, "This man's killed one of your own hoping to finish me! Would you have him wearing the Captain's hat?"

Sparks sneered. "This from the man who scoffs at Truth?"

"The Cap's speaking straight and I be the one that knows," cried Andi. 'Twas Ben left the system running when he jumped ship so he could send his mind to Piel and Ling. The system was ticking like a fine clock when I bought the earring and it sent Ben's mind to me along with his killing." She nodded toward Piel and Ling. "And the faces of his killers!"

Piel and Ling were watching, listening. Ling said matter-of-factly, "We *will* want the girl."

"Aye, you hear that, Sparks? So put a thought to it! You cut my neck, you kill the head that's on it, and what do you know but half the system? It's Ben's in my head, and Ben knows the whole of it."

"Meaning . . . " said the Captain, "take away the girl and the whole matter ends." The Captain shifted his aim so Andi could see right down the bore. "You know half the system, Sparks, but she knows all of it. You know how to scramble it, but she knows how to fix it. Without her, the system's no good . . . and neither is your deal, and what does The Gate go away with?"

Sparks tightened his grip on her. "Give it up, Thatch. You can't do it."

"Ask Jean-Pierre." The Captain's voice was low and even. "You were there. You know I can. You know I will."

THE BATTLE

Lighter in hand, I reached to ignite the vent hole of the cannon.

Scalarag blocked me. "This isn't it."

I nearly struck him. "Isn't what?"

"The moment."

"*What* moment?"

"You'll know. Keep an eye on 'em. Gotta go below, fire up the engines."

I'll know?

* * *

The Captain called out to his men as he aimed his pistol at Andi's head. "You've all sailed with me, so what say you? What rule's to stop me? From what

Truth comes the shame?"

He waited, looked them in the eyes. Not a single man gave an answer. Andi began to tremble.

The Captain called again, "Can you not tell me? Where's the wrong in taking the girl's life?"

One wimpy little swab offered, "We don't get the money . . . "

A whiny little murmur of agreement passed through the crew.

The Captain watched them a moment, gave them time, but all he got was silence.

At last, with resignation, he raised the muzzle of his pistol toward the sky and uncocked the hammer. "So . . . if there be a Truth, it's of a truth that you have none, and *I* took it from you. Very well, then. Let the Truth fall to me, and *I'll* be the man." He tucked the pistol into his belt, then removed his hat and held it high. "Sparks is your captain!"

No one cheered.

"Hip! Hip!"

Two said Hurray.

"Hip! Hip!"

Same two.

Sparks' hands were occupied holding and threatening Andi. Thatch did the honors, placing the hat on Sparks' head. He then took hold of Andi and pulled her gently away–

As Sparks went berserk! He screamed, his eyes rolled, he held his head as if it were bursting; he toppled, rolled on the ground. The hat came off, but it had done it's work: Sparks would never be clever or conniving again.

Captain Thatch snatched up the hat and, before putting it back on, surreptitiously removed the earring he'd concealed in the lining. He dropped the earring, crushed it under his boot, and replaced his hat.

* * *

This was it! The moment! I knew!

Running, I touched fire to the vent hole of Cannon One, then Two, then Three. Each gun unleashed a fiery, percussive thunder, recoiling against its tethers; the explosions quaked my insides; the whole ship rocked under my feet.

The town square disappeared behind a cloud of blue smoke and oat-colored haze.

* * *

The Captain knew the moment as well. He held Andi tightly against him, his back to the blast, as three boxes worth of Cheerios, reduced to crumbles and dust, blasted the whole village like a sandstorm. The stuff got into eyes, stung faces, threw everyone into a panic.

Which was just what Thatch wanted. "Run, lass, run!"

Andi kicked off her parrot feet and sprinted for the wharf, winged arms covering her face through the rain of oats. The Captain, face sheltered under his hat, stayed right at her heels. Passing the photo booth, Andi grabbed a scarf from the rack of Readers, then dashed onto the wharf and up the gangplank.

"Cast off, cast off!" Thatch shouted, stomping up the gangplank behind her.

* * *

Scalarag had already drilled me on casting off the lines. I cast off the last stern line even as Andi and the Captain landed on the deck.

"The system's yours, lass," I heard the Captain say as he threw off the gangplank.

Andi did a strange thing: she ran up to me and handed me the scarf. "Here, put this one on!" Then she dashed below.

A Reader, no doubt. A signal for help? I took off my old scarf and put on the new one.

The smoke was clearing. Some of Thatch's crew were occupied with Sparks who was leaping on the tables, waving his knife around, throwing things. The others were scattered like windfall about the town square, bereft of a leader — or a moral imperative.

Ling was filled with purpose, however. I could see all of his rogues running our way, some squinting and teary-eyed from the powdered oats, some clear-eyed enough to fire their weapons. Bullets pinged and chipped the bulwarks, the companion. I crawled for any cover I could find as the engines below rumbled and the big hull lurched away from the wharf.

* * *

Below, Andi tapped out lines of command and code at the console. Once again, the computer beeped, drives whirred to life, and the very attractive lady pirate appeared on the screen, presenting a menu of links and sub-pages.

Ready.

* * *

"Oh!" said Audrey Snow, viewing the screen in Key West.

"Oh my word," said Zedekiah, seeing what she saw. "Oh my word!"

Tank, Brenda, and Daniel came running from different parts of the house.

Zedekiah was ecstatic. "The system has unscrambled, and not only that, it's let us in! We're getting a signal from one of the Readers!"

"Way cool!" said Tank.

And that was the last thing said before they all stared at each other, thinking the same thing.

Tank looked at Brenda, then Daniel. "I'll do it."

Audrey picked up the earring. "How can we be sure?"

"Everything looks stable," said Zedekiah. "Only . . . good heavens! The Reader must be aboard a speedboat. I've never seen a sailing ship go so fast!"

Tank didn't have pierced ears. He just pressed the earring against his ear. His eyes widened with shock. "Whoa! WHOA!" He backed off, staring at the earring in his hand.

Zedekiah got quite a scare. "Hello? Are you still with us? What is your name? Do you know where you are?"

"I'm Matt Damon," he answered. "Just kidding. I'm okay, but boy, what a ride!" He pressed the earring against his head again. "Man oh MAN!" He almost lost his balance. Audrey and Brenda guided him to a chair. He jerked, he leaned, he ducked as if the chair were a toboggan at the Olympics. "Woo-hooo! We are *flying!*"

* * *

Well, of course Tank was inside my head, standing next to Captain Thatch aboard the *Predator* as the ship defied its design and anyone's good sense, plowing through the water at reckless, breakneck speed, lurching with nauseating power over the swells and kicking up a violent wake. The shrouds were humming, the masts and yards groaning.

Thatch gripped the wheel, a strange, gleeful look on his face as he pointed the bow toward a small island a mile away. "Bindy's Mayday, they call it! Very nice channel on the other side with little room for ships to pass! Let 'em follow us there!"

I looked astern. Not more than a mile back, the *Riqueza* was giving chase. Apparently, it had oversized engine power as well; it was keeping up.

* * *

"This ain't real!" said Tank, seeing one three-masted ship from the deck of another, plowing along with a bone in its teeth though its sails were furled. "It's the pirate show, but we didn't see this part."

"Whose thoughts and impressions are you receiving?" Snow wanted to know.

I was trying to talk some sense to this loony pirate before he got us all killed, all the while gaining new insight into where the stereotypical sailor got his language.

"Uh . . . angry, scolding, kind of know-it-all . . . " said Tank. "Big words . . . whoa! Bad words too." He grinned with recognition. "It's the professor."

* * *

Thatch grabbed me. "Take the wheel."

Horrors! The man was daffy! "I will do no such thing!"

"Trust your captain!" He pulled me over and put my hands on the wheel. "She likes to bear away to starboard without her sails. Make her mind. Circle to the right of that rock sticking up, just to the right of Bindy's, you see it?"

I was holding the reins of a bucking monster, fighting for control. I nodded as if we were having a reasonable conversation.

"Stay clear of it, then duck behind the island and into the channel. Scalarag's giving you full throttle."

"Full — !?"

* * *

"Whoa!" Tank laughed. "He is scared poop-less! Sorry . . . "

* * *

The Captain raised his spyglass to his eye. "Aye, it's Ling's men, all right. They won't let us get away, no way in heaven or hell." He set the spyglass aside and headed for the companion, leaving me alone at the wheel.

"What are you going to do?" I hollered over my shoulder, my hands welded to the wheel.

"The right thing, if God be my Judge," was all he said as he went down the stairs to his quarters.

The rock to the right of Bindy's Mayday was a black, jagged tooth, a perfect hull opener. I veered farther to the right to be sure we missed it, then cut a gradual turn to port to head around the island. Now I could see another island beyond this one, and between them, a narrow channel. I steered for the channel and, looking back, saw the *Riqueza* had veered to port to circle the island from the other direction.

They were going to head us off.

* * *

Zedekiah Snow activated another computer, another program, and a real time map of the Caribbean appeared with a tiny blip representing the location of the Reader. "Well folks, there it is."

Tank remained in the chair, eyes closed, experiencing the lurching and dashing of the *Predator*, the wind in my face, the salt spray in my eyes, the roar of the wind in the rigging — and the *Riqueza* rounding the other end of the island to intercept us. "He's not having fun. There's something really heavy going down."

Brenda stood. "We've got to get down there!"

Tank pulled the earring away from his head, blinked to get his own senses back, and said, "Andi's grandpa! He's got a jet, a chopper, probably has a boat!"

Brenda grabbed her cell phone.

* * *

"So you've found your friends, whoever they be?"

Andi was startled to hear the Captain's voice behind her, but not alarmed. By now it was clear the Captain knew it all: the inquiry from another system, the access code, her responding, and of course her fitting me with a Reader scarf to send a signal to whoever it was. "I think it's them."

The Captain stepped up and looked over her shoulder. "Look at the tag on the inquiry. You've been queried by someone in Florida." He laughed. "And I can name that party in one guess: Zedekiah Snow! Your friends are in good hands. Come to think of it, so are you! Be assured, lass, they know where you are. Here, put this on." He offered her an inflatable life vest.

The way the ship was rocking and pounding, the vest seemed to her an entirely good idea. She put it on.

"Now I need you topside."

* * *

"For you, professor," came the Captain's voice over the roar of the wind.

The Captain had returned with Andi and was offering an inflatable life vest. As he took the wheel, I slipped on the vest and clipped it tight.

"AH!" he laughed, sighting the *Riqueza* at the far

end of the channel and closing fast. "Piel's thinking hasn't changed. He's at the helm of that boat with Ling at his side, no doubt, and doing what I thought! So how's your Honor, professor? How's your Truth?"

The face I made must have been hideous. "I fail to see how that pertains to our situation!"

The Captain grinned, amused, which I did not find amusing. "So we never talked about it, or you weren't listening? It's all come down to the rules, and it's time to face it: Wherever it comes from, we'll need a little Honor . . . in our situation."

"I would prefer a level head and better driving."

"Oh, would you now?"

He reached for the engine telegraph and signaled Scalarag to ease the engines back to Dead Slow Ahead, the first sane choice he'd made thus far, in my estimation. The *Predator* slowed, although I noticed the *Riqueza* did not.

"Well," I started to say, still eyeing the *Riqueza*. "a reasonable first step—"

Andi screamed. I turned just in time to see the Captain holding her aloft as she kicked and struggled, making his way to the rail.

What — ?

NO! I ran, with no other thought than to get her out of his hands.

Too late! Thatch threw her over the side! I reached the railing only to see her splash into the waves. Her life vest triggered and inflated, bearing her back to the surface where she splashed helplessly, the moving ship leaving her in its wake.

I was about to leap in after her when something bumped me. "I suppose you'll be wanting this?" said the Captain.

He was offering me a bulky package, rather heavy. The label read "Life Raft." With no hesitation I clutched the package to my chest, swung my legs over the rail, and dropped into the sea.

I was still beneath the surface, eyes shut in a grimace and breath held, when the water triggered my life vest and the raft and they inflated, the life vest hugging me as I popped to the surface and the life raft unfolding and forming within my reach. I grabbed on and clambered in, blinking the sting of salt from my eyes as I searched the expansive waters for Andi.

There! I could see the yellow flotation around her neck, the redness of her hair. She was so distant, so minuscule, bobbing, intermittently vanishing between the swells. But she was waving. She was safe.

* * *

The roar of the *Predator*, again at full throttle, was fading in the distance. I turned to see Thatch looking back and giving a farewell wave, satisfied, no doubt, that we would be all right. Then he looked ahead, closing on the *Riqueza* as if he fully intended to ram her.

Which, I still marvel to report, he did. I suppose Piel, at the helm of the *Riqueza*, expected him to turn tail and run, or perhaps shoot it out, or surrender, being so outgunned. But Thatch would not turn away, nor would he slow down. With cunning and skill, he even anticipated every evasive maneuver the *Riqueza* made, staying in her path no matter what she did.

First came the ball of fire and the flying debris — lumber, splinters, canvas and rigging exploding skyward — and then, a second or two later, the roar and shock of the explosion. I was transfixed. Stunned.

"Hey!" Andi called. She was kicking and paddling my way.

I assembled a plastic oar that came with the life raft and paddled toward her, all the while staring over my shoulder, trying to fathom what I'd just seen, even when nothing remained but steaming embers on the water.

Epilogue

With both of us paddling the life raft, Andi and I easily made the sandy beach of Bindy's Mayday, and it was the need to de-pressurize, I imagine, to make some sense of all that had happened, that launched us back into the discussion we started on the *Barbee Jay* but never finished: was there an ultimate Truth and therefore a basis for Right and Wrong, and was the existence of God necessary for such a Truth to exist? What happened aboard the *Predator*, from our being kidnapped to the horrendous destruction we barely avoided in the channel, amounted to a practical experiment. The devil was in the data, of course, and our differing interpretations. As a result, three hours passed as mere minutes, the intensity of our debate broken only by the sound of an approaching airplane.

"Hey!" Andi cried, "it's the *Silver Lady*!"

It was the nickname given to her grandfather's

floatplane. We could see Tank, Brenda, and Daniel waving from the plane's windows as it set down in the channel like a big, aluminum goose.

I thought it best to wrap up our discussion before we rowed out to the plane. I granted her the possibility—since it brought her comfort—that nature, physics, and morality could make sense because there was a Superior Mind behind it all; she granted me the fact that, despite the danger and with no thought of what a supposed God might require, I still jumped into the sea to save her.

As for the Captain . . . though I assumed he'd acted upon a spark of good in his own nature, Andi preferred to think our being there may have fanned that spark to life. Well . . . either way, I suppose.

But most of all, I summarized feelings I felt no need to explain. "All things considered," I said to my assistant, "I am boundlessly glad and relieved that you're safe."

She smiled and nodded. "Same here."

* * *

I'll close my recounting of the tale with a certainty and an *un*certainty.

The certainty: Zedekiah Snow was a decent fellow — at least, as one such as myself might measure such a quality as "decent" — and knew his own technology well enough to isolate memories and impressions in any brain that were not native to that brain. In Andi's case, he quickly identified the memories and impressions of Ben Cardiff and neutralized them in a two second treatment. Andi is well again, no longer plagued by any past tampering with her mind.

The *un*certainty: While we were lifting off from the channel, we flew over the blackened debris field where the two ships collided and saw on the nearest shore a familiar little craft: the *Predator's* wooden boat that first carried Andi and I to the ship. It couldn't have gotten there unless someone had rowed it. Had the Captain granted Scalarag a dismissal to safety as he had granted us? To add to that, the ships were quite a distance away, too far to tell if Captain Horatio Thatch was still on board when they exploded.

At any rate, neither man has ever been found to our knowledge . . . and perhaps that was the whole intention.

A strange thing, Honor. I'm sure more discussions will follow.

Fair winds.

Don't miss the other books in the Harbingers series wich can be purchased separately or in collections:

CYCLE ONE: INVITATION
The Call,
The House,
The Sentinels,
The Girl.

CYCLE TWO: MOSAIC
The Revealing
Infestation

Infiltration
The Fog

CYCLE THREE (in progress)
Leviathan
The Mind Pirates